Maggie froze

Dare she turn her hand over, let his shaft rest against her palm? She wanted to, yet she wasn't sure she had the courage.

"Do you want to touch me, Maggie?" Cord asked hoarsely.

She swallowed and nodded, but couldn't seem to move.

He trailed his fingertips over her knuckles, his touch a light dusting. "Have you ever seen a man naked before?"

She widened her eyes at the outlandish notion, briefly met his gaze before hers flickered away. "No."

He picked up her hand and turned it over, palm up. To her amazement, his hand wasn't too steady. It made it easier to look at him, see the unexpected vulnerability in his face. See the slight tremble of his shoulders. He was actually trembling. Why? And then she met his eyes.

Without looking away from her, he lifted her hand to his lips and kissed her palm, and then he wrapped her fingers around his smooth, hot manhood. She jumped at the initial touch, as if he'd scorched her, and then watched in awe as the trembling in his shoulders spread through his chest.

Dear Reader,

It's my hope that by now you've read about the fantastical journey of the two Winslow sisters, Reese and Ellie, in *Once an Outlaw* and *Once a Gambler.* The heroines and readers were transported to 1870s Deadwood. Now, in *Once a Rebel,* we return there with Cord Braddock, an ex-stuntman turned private detective who is searching for the two women. Since Cord is half Navajo Indian, the challenges he faces extend beyond traveling through time and falling for a virginal heroine.

Although I'm currently working on a contemporary story, I really hope there are more time-travel romances in my future. Hmm, I'm thinking logging in the Pacific Northwest or maybe even the early frontier of Alaska? Sometimes my mind is a dangerous place. Sure keeps me entertained, though. I hope this story does the same for you.

Happy reading!

Debbi Rawlins

Once A Rebel

DEBBI RAWLINS

HARLEQUIN®

TORONTO • NEW YORK • LONDON
AMSTERDAM • PARIS • SYDNEY • HAMBURG
STOCKHOLM • ATHENS • TOKYO • MILAN • MADRID
PRAGUE • WARSAW • BUDAPEST • AUCKLAND

Recycling programs
for this product may
not exist in your area.

ISBN-13: 978-0-373-79471-3
ISBN-10:   0-373-79471-1

ONCE A REBEL

www.eHarlequin.com

Printed in U.S.A.

ABOUT THE AUTHOR

Debbi Rawlins lives in central Utah, out in the country, surrounded by woods and deer and wild turkeys. It's quite a change for a city girl, who didn't even know where the state of Utah was until four years ago. Of course, unfamiliarity never stopped her. Between her junior and senior years of college she spontaneously left home in Hawaii and bummed around Europe for five weeks by herself. And much to her parents' delight, she returned home with only a quarter in her wallet.

Books by Debbi Rawlins

HARLEQUIN BLAZE
13—IN HIS WILDEST DREAMS
36—EDUCATING GINA
60—HANDS ON
112—ANYTHING GOES...
143—HE'S ALL THAT*
160—GOOD TO BE BAD
183—A GLIMPSE OF FIRE
220—HOT SPOT**
250—THE HONEYMOON
      THAT WASN'T*
312—SLOW HAND LUKE*
351—IF HE ONLY KNEW...*
368—WHAT SHE
      REALLY WANTS
      FOR CHRISTMAS†
417—ALL OR NOTHING
455—ONCE AN OUTLAW††

 *Men To Do
**Do Not Disturb
†Million Dollar Secrets
††Stolen from Time

Don't miss any of our special offers. Write to us at the following address for information on our newest releases.

Harlequin Reader Service
U.S.: 3010 Walden Ave., P.O. Box 1325, Buffalo, NY 14269
Canadian: P.O. Box 609, Fort Erie, Ont. L2A 5X3

I would like to acknowledge that *Once a Rebel* is a work of fiction and meant solely to entertain. While I have paid close attention to historical detail, now and then I may have stretched the facts for the sake of the story.

1

"Mad Dog Manson still in the wind?" Cord Braddock asked casually as he pocketed the much-needed check he'd just received for his last job. Another messy divorce case. Yeah, the guy was cheating, and Cord had delivered the proof that would net the soon-to-be ex-wife a nice settlement. But if he had to spy on one more sleazy, lying dirtbag husband, he was gonna...

"No."

"Who caught him?" His gaze shot to Leslie's impassive face.

"No, you can't have the job." Slowly, she shook her head, her blue gaze firm and unwavering. Behind her on the beige office wall was a poster from one of her earliest movies.

"So no one else has bagged him yet." Now, that was some serious money to be made. Enough for five months' rent, five lease payments on Cord's Porsche and next year's gym membership.

"You're a private detective, not a bounty hunter, and even if you were, I wouldn't give you this one." Leslie slid open her desk drawer and pulled out a strongbox where he knew she kept petty cash. "This is Manson's third strike. He's not coming in without taking down anything that moves."

Yeah, Cord had his P.I. license now, even a gun and permit to carry it, but calling him a private detective was being too generous with the kind of jobs he'd been doing. "I'm not looking for easy."

"You should be." She gestured with a lift of her chin. "How's the shoulder?"

"I want Mad Dog, Leslie." Out of habit, or because she'd called attention to it, he flexed his injured shoulder. Today it didn't hurt too much. "I'm dead serious about this."

She leaned back in her creamy yellow leather chair and stared at him with a sympathy he found hard to stomach. Yet she wasn't that unlike him. Chewed up and spit out by Hollywood when her use and youth had hit a wall. Still, she'd done okay for herself, invested well while she'd been making some dough, and then bought old man Barker's detective and bail bonds agency.

Cord hadn't been so smart. He'd spent the considerable money he'd made as a stuntman on cars and women as fast as he pulled in paychecks, too caught up in the good life to see that inevitably it would come to a crashing end. He pushed up from the too-small chair facing her and stretched out his legs. Nice office, but more chic than practical. Not that he knew anything about practicality. If he did, he'd give up the Porsche.

"Come on, Leslie," he said smoothly, giving her his best pleading puppy-dog eyes.

Leslie sighed. "No."

Cord exhaled sharply and looked out the window at the blue California sky, marred only by the persistent gray smog that hung over the Valley. Maybe it was time to move. L.A. was expensive and crowded and toxic. But where would he go? Not back to Arizona. Certainly not back to the reservation. The mere thought sent a shaft of dread down his spine. He'd go back to begging on the streets of L.A. before he'd end up there again.

"I need work, Les, but not this nickel-and-dime stuff."

"Even the small stuff pays the bills."

Cord drove a hand through his hair. It was long. Too long.

Bad enough being six-three since his size made it hard to blend in when he did surveillance. Looking like the half-Indian he was didn't help matters. "Don't worry about my shoulder. I'm back to bench-pressing three times a week. I'm fine."

"Right." Her mouth twisted wryly. "That's why the studios are pounding down your door to offer you work."

He gritted his teeth, angry, but worse, a heartbeat away from panic. A year had passed since the accident and he still didn't have full range of motion. One more injury, the doctor had said, and Cord's arm would be totally useless. "It's an insurance issue. It doesn't mean squat."

"Hell, Cord, make peace with it already," she said, annoyance flashing in her eyes. "You're out of the stunt business. For good. Got it? You're thirty-three, which isn't so bad, granted, but with your shoulder hanging on by a thread, there will be no more plum jobs. Not the kind that used to pay for your Porsche. For God's sake, we don't even know half the guys calling the shots anymore. You understand as well as I do how this town works, you've got to know somebody. You've already been replaced, my friend. Deal with it."

She was right. That's what stunk. It didn't matter that he still worked out six days a week, that he was strong and fit and had a unique look that had once earned him top dollar when westerns had made a comeback. It meant nothing that he'd never balked at a single stunt they'd asked him to do. The more dangerous, the more willing he'd been to take on the challenge. The truth was, a year out of the business, coupled with an injury that made him a liability, and he was forgotten.

"All the more reason I need better gigs than chasing after scumbag husbands. I need some credibility if I want to make it as a private detective and attract worthwhile clients."

"You're absolutely right." She looked pleased, obviously

having bought his line of crap. "That's why I have a proposition for you."

"I'm listening."

"The Winslow case. The sisters are still missing."

"Not exactly a news flash." The daughters of actors Brad and Linea Winslow, a Hollywood powerhouse couple, had bizarrely disappeared within six months of each other. Like vultures feasting on roadkill, the media had been all over the story. Until some upcoming young actor had shoved his male lover off the hill below the Hollywood sign.

"Other than the FBI and Malcolm Baxter, who I hear the Winslows have kept on retainer, I doubt many people are working the case at this point. It's been too long and costly."

Malcolm Baxter. The smug, condescending bastard. The guy's name alone was enough to make Cord's insides clench. Everything about the older man—from his Armani suits to his trademark tasseled Italian loafers—made Cord want to teach the guy a lesson. It wasn't the man's success Cord begrudged, but something in his penetrating soulless eyes that seemed to remind Cord of every humiliation he'd suffered since the day he'd left the reservation.

He forced away thoughts of Baxter. "What's it been, a year and a half since they went missing?"

"Nineteen months, to be exact." She reached behind and swung her black designer purse off the gleaming mahogany credenza that matched her desk. She set down the fancy bag and fished out a small key.

Yep, Leslie had grown to like nice things. Just like him. Difference was, she could afford them. "According to news reports, the trail went cold fast," he said, watching her unlock the strongbox. "I don't think the police picked up a single lead. Not even when the second sister went missing. Even the FBI turned up nothing."

"That's right. The mystery of the century some reporters were calling it." She took out a wad of cash and looked up at him, her blue eyes sparkling with excitement. "Imagine the publicity when someone finally finds them. I mean, they couldn't have both vanished into thin air. They have to be somewhere." She gave a small shrug. "Even if it's just their bodies that turn up."

He waited for her to finish, and then finally got her meaning. "And you think—" He shook his head in disbelief. At the time, the best in the business had taken up the search. Private dicks and bounty hunters from all over the country had crawled out from under rocks and descended on the vacant house the women had inherited in Deadwood, South Dakota, and where each had last been seen, in hopes of claiming the reward. Even tabloid reporters had dived into the frenzy. Everyone had come up empty. "You're nuts."

"You wanted credibility. Not even considering the million bucks the Winslows are offering to locate their daughters, find them and you'd be able to write your own ticket. You'd be in so much demand, you wouldn't even need me."

"I can't afford to go on a wild-goose chase. You know that. Not to mention the expense of traveling all the way to Deadwood. I need a paying job."

"That's why I'm willing to stake you."

Cord briefly eyed the cash. Two stacks. Made up of hundreds. Temptation pulled at his gut. "Why?"

"For half the reward money, and publicity for my agency."

"So why the sudden interest?" he asked, waiting for her to squirm. This was a bunch of crap. They both knew it.

She didn't even blink. "Because the Deadwood house has been sold. The new owner is tearing part of it down and having some extensive renovation done to the rest of the building in order to turn it into a bed-and-breakfast. This may be the last chance to uncover any clues."

He still didn't buy her motive. "The Winslows sold the house when it's their last link to their daughters? That doesn't make sense."

"I couldn't agree more." The corners of Leslie's mouth quirked. "But I heard that the almighty Malcolm Baxter convinced them that the place was a dead end. Probably got a kickback from the Realtor for convincing them."

Cord knew she'd never liked Baxter, either. Whatever her reasons, he wasn't sure. Probably had more to do with professional rivalry since the guy was a shameless publicity whore and managed to snag the best clients. Cord's dislike went deeper, and Leslie, the conniving little witch, was using Baxter to play Cord. "What makes you think I can do what no one else could?" Grudgingly, because the man did have an uncanny knack for closing a case, he added, "Including the almighty Baxter."

"You're good at tracking."

Cord smiled in spite of himself. Coming from anyone else he would have found the remark a snide commentary on his being half-Navajo. Hell, too bad it hadn't come from Baxter. It would've been Cord's perfect excuse to pop the guy. Show everyone just how good his shoulder had healed, at the same time send the smug bastard halfway to hell. But someone like Baxter was far too slick and cunning to be an open bigot. Especially not here in good old liberal Hollywood.

Unlike some of the townspeople who lived near the reservation. When the economy was down, there were folks who accused the "dirty, rotten Indians" of taking their jobs, taking food out of the mouths of their children. Cord had been a blameless child himself when he'd crossed into their world. But they'd dragged him through the mud, spat in his face, shaved off his long black hair.

Had circumstances been different when they'd first met,

Baxter could've been any one of those men. Cord knew the truth of that deep in his gut. He saw it in Baxter's eyes. They reminded Cord of a past he wanted to forget, pure and simple.

But he wouldn't let that distract him now. Leslie was right, he was damn good at tracking, but the idea that he could make headway on the high-profile case was ridiculous. He knew exactly what this was about. The sparkling eyes, the phony excitement in her voice, all a nice touch. But of course she'd been a decent enough actress at one time.

"If I'm so good at tracking, why can't I go after Mad Dog," he reminded her. "That could net us each a nice payoff."

Leslie sighed with disgust. "Let it go, Braddock. I'm not helping you cripple yourself for life." She flipped through the first stack of hundred-dollar bills, as if mentally counting, but he had a feeling she had something else on her mind. "You still seeing Brenda Carlisle?"

"Occasionally. Why?"

Leslie's lips curved in a rueful smile. "This town isn't good for you anymore, Cord. Some friendly advice? Get the hell out while you still can."

He knew she meant well. Brenda was just like the rest of the women in his circle, a circle getting smaller by the day. She was a taker. And lately he had less to give. He shouldn't resent Leslie's concern. She was the closest person he had to a friend. He did, anyway.

Clutching the back of the leather guest chair, he watched her lay the two stacks of bills on her desk and then slowly push them toward him.

Hesitating, he tightened his grip. The late afternoon sun filtered through the tinted window and caught his watch. The gold gleamed under the beam of sunlight. Damn, he didn't want to have to pawn it again.

Cord clenched his jaw, and reached for the money. Only a

year ago he'd been sitting on top of the world, his phone ringing off the hook with job offers and A-list party invitations. Then one wrecked shoulder and it had all come to this. His pride was as fragile as the colored beads his grandmother had strung to keep food on their table. And here he was, accepting charity.

2

SHE WAS A SLY ONE, that Leslie. Cord shook his head as he sank to the edge of his bed, irrationally annoyed at the plushness of the burgundy comforter his interior decorator had insisted upon, and pulled off his boots. Not only had Leslie slipped him enough money to pay next month's rent, but she'd also effectively stopped him from chasing down Mad Dog.

The guy was big and mean but dumb as they came. Wearily, his gaze went to the leather duffel bag sitting on the floor near his walk-in closet. He still hadn't checked on flights to Deadwood. Going there would appease Leslie, but be a huge waste of his time. He laughed humorlessly. Time was about the only thing he had lately. No money. No prospects. Just a hoity-toity apartment he could no longer afford.

He could downsize, get a cheaper one bedroom in Culver City. Unload some of the furniture through one of those fancy consignment shops. Getting rid of some of this stuff wouldn't kill him. But the Porsche…

Man, he loved that car.

Even after two years he got a kick out of how valet parkers rushed to the curb when he pulled up. Nah, the car was a deal breaker. He had to do whatever it took to keep her.

He kicked his boots in the direction of the armoire, and then lay back and closed his eyes. The air conditioner kicked on with a low hum and he knew he should get up and close the window. Better yet, turn off the air. Eighteen years he'd been away from the reservation and he still hadn't acquired a taste for the indoors. He liked an actual breeze skimming his face.

Summers on the reservation had been hotter than hell itself. Burning wood to cook hadn't helped. Come winter, the mountain of wood Cord kept chopped and the scratchy handmade wool blankets were the only things that kept them warm. His grandmother never complained. Not even when, at seven, Cord had been dropped at her doorstep because his mother had died in a car accident and his father didn't want to be saddled with a kid.

Cord never thought about his old man, but his grandmother, Masi, he still missed. Diabetes stole her from him two days after he'd turned fifteen. The image of his grandmother's cold limp body came unbidden and he ruthlessly dismissed it. He'd been clutching her hand for over an hour before his friend Bobby Blackhawk had found him huddled next to her corpse.

The next day Cord had left the reservation. Hadn't even waited for her burial. Even now, years later, he couldn't figure out why and the thought still got to him. There was nothing in his useless life he'd regretted more than missing her funeral. Not even the fact that he hadn't finished high school and hadn't gotten his GED until he was twenty-two. And only then because he'd been badgered into it by Madeleine Sweeney. But he'd owed the woman. Big-time. Owed her his life, probably.

After three harsh years in L.A., she'd been the first person to really give a damn about him. Sure, he'd tackled the guy who tried ripping off her purse at the sidewalk bistro where she'd been lunching and Cord had been busing tables. But she'd had megabucks and an important producer husband, and she could've just as easily given Cord her thanks instead of the introduction that led to his lucrative job as a stuntman.

Sadly, he *had* attended her funeral last year. The emotional ceremony and church full of mourners had brought up a whole mess of shit he didn't want to think about. He rolled over onto his stomach, a sudden image of his grandmother's brown face wreathed in a smile so vivid his breath caught.

He opened his eyes, blinked and then squeezed them shut again, burying his face deeper into the soft comforter.

That had been happening a lot lately. Fleeting memories of her that unsettled him. Last month he'd even foolishly thought he'd caught a glimpse of her standing near a street vendor's cart on Olvera Street. Madeleine's untimely death had obviously kicked up a lot of guilt no matter how much he reasoned with himself that he hadn't actually abandoned Masi. She'd been dead. Gone. Before he'd ever set foot off the reservation.

If anything, she'd abandoned him.

The crazy thought came out of nowhere. She hadn't chosen to leave him. If she'd had it in her power to stay, she would've protected him from the hate and bigotry he encountered after he'd left the Dine. If she hadn't died, he may never have left at all.

Funny, as a rebellious teen he'd ridiculed the language and customs of the Dine, but even today he thought of them in terms of the Navajo word they called themselves. Dine. The People. It came as naturally to him as breathing. Without resentment. Without judgment.

Besides, he'd never had any quarrel with the Dine. He had some fond memories of days spent swimming in the river and fishing with Bobby Blackhawk, sleeping outside under the stars and sitting around a campfire repeating old Navajo legends they'd heard from the elders.

But he didn't kid himself that he would've been content to stay on the reservation even if his grandmother had lived longer. At fourteen, he'd started getting restless, curious about life outside of his sheltered existence. But at fifteen, he'd been ill-prepared to face adult realities.

On cold lonely nights, his only comfort had been the secret fantasy that he'd once again meet Masi. That maybe she'd traveled to California ahead of him and had been busy setting up a home for them.

He smiled at the memory, reached for one of the pillows propped up against the headboard. By her own belief, the Navajo belief, a spirit never truly died but went on to another life in another place. Naturally he thought that was a bunch of crap—when your time was up, everything went black. No more second chances. Dirt to dirt pretty much summed it up.

He flopped onto his back again and slipped the pillow under his head. Out of the corner of his eye, he caught a glimpse of the duffel bag. Damn it, he had to make up his mind about the Winslow business. Deadwood was a hell of a long way to go for nothing.

CORD OPENED HIS EYES and jackknifed off the bed, his heart hammering his chest. The room was almost black, except for the light from the pool's reflection intermittently swirling in through the slanted blinds. He stared at the window, still open several inches, and listened. There was only silence now. And his own ragged breathing.

It was a dream. Just a crazy dream.

His pulse slowed as his eyes grew more accustomed to the darkness. How long had he slept? His gaze went to the alarm clock on the nightstand. The glowing red numbers told him it was just after midnight. He swung his feet to the floor, feeling shaky from the events of the dream. Not that he remembered much, only fractured bits of recollection filtered past the fog of sleep. No mistake, the dream had been about Masi.

Normally when he dreamt of his grandmother, he felt comforted. Not tonight. The edginess that crawled over his nerve endings wouldn't cease. He closed his eyes again, trying desperately to recall more of the dream. He stretched his neck from side to side, trying to ease the tension, as if he could shake loose a memory.

They'd been sitting at their cook fire on the reservation, that much he remembered. Except they were outside and the sun was beginning to set. His age was fuzzy, and Masi looked like she always had—slightly stooped, leathery skin, old before her time. An eagle soared overhead and she'd pointed skyward…and then…

Cord exhaled sharply, and opened his eyes. That's all he could remember. Frustrated, he pushed up from the bed. The wavering light from the pool caught on the outline of a dark lump sitting between the armoire and the closet. He strained to make out what it was. The black leather duffel.

That's all it took. Memories of the dream washed over him. The eagle turning into a plane, golden sunlight gilding by the distant hills, the Black Hills, just like in the travel agency brochures. He knew suddenly, deep down in his gut. Masi had plainly told him to go to Deadwood.

Too bad, Cord thought as he stopped the car in front of the Deadwood property. The house was huge, two and a half, maybe three stories, with a big porch facing the west where you could sit and watch the sun go down. The main door was off center, a peculiarity he kind of liked. He wondered which part of the house they were tearing down.

The new owner, who was a developer, had had it with both freelance detectives and reporters, according to his secretary. She'd stopped short of giving Cord a key but she made sure he understood the place was currently deserted and, with a flashing dimple, subtly let him know that the kitchen door was likely to be unlocked. He'd promised the cute little blonde a quiet dinner.

Why not? How much time would it take to find out this case was a dead end? After waiting in crowded airports and then enduring two choppy flights, the whimsy of last night's dream had worn thin. So had his patience. The blonde would prove a nice distraction tonight. What was her name…? Sue—slightly younger and shorter than he liked them, but she was eager.

He probed his aching shoulder and took a deep breath against the cramping pain. Flying coach was a bitch for someone as tall and broad as he was, but he had to make the cash Leslie had given him last as long as possible. He had every intention of paying her back the amount he'd siphoned off for rent, and whatever he spent on dinner tonight, but the rest was gonna be on her nickel for sending him on this fool's errand.

After following the side of the house, he spied the kitchen through a bare bay window. With the toe of his black snakeskin boots, he carefully picked his way through some debris to the stoop.

Just like Sue had said, the door was unlocked. Good, they couldn't get him on breaking, only entering. He smiled wryly, and unnecessarily touched the butt of his gun through his sport jacket. He didn't need the piece. Transporting it had been more trouble than it was worth. But who knew? Maybe he could finish his business here and still pick up Mad Dog's trail. General consensus was that the guy had left L.A. and headed east. Cord only needed to swing south to cross his path.

As soon as Cord stepped over the threshold, a cloud of particle-board dust assailed his nostrils. Coughing, he waved a hand to clear the air. The kitchen had been torn apart, the appliances ripped from the wall, half of it already gone, allowing him to see into what must have been a dining room. Only the chandelier and ripped wallpaper remained.

Shaking his head, he walked through the room into another and faced much of the same. No furniture, just big empty spaces, barely contained by walls left with gaping holes and framed by dull peeling paint. The scuffed wood floors didn't look too bad, there were a few warped floorboards, but that was pretty much it. He shouldn't be wasting his time here.

Then he noticed the stairs guided by a carved dark cherry banister that ended in two ornate scrolls, and wondered why the workmen hadn't protected the wood. Surely they would try to salvage this piece. Although his tastes veered to the contemporary end of the spectrum, even he could appreciate the fine craftsmanship.

Without thinking, he ran his palm over the smooth wood and an odd sensation of familiarity washed over him. It called to mind the many times as a kid that he'd watched the elders carve figures of animals to be sold at souvenir shops. Samuel Wauneka had offered to teach him the dying art, and Cord had balked. He hadn't thought about that in a long time, either.

Cord started up toward the landing, briefly considering if it was worth the risk of checking the second floor.

Not in the hope of finding a lead, but out of simple curiosity. Before he'd consciously made a decision, he tested the stability of the first step. Seemed solid enough for his weight. The workers had to get up there somehow, so he wasn't too concerned.

The stairs turned out to be surprisingly solid, but not so the internal walls upstairs. On the left side of the house, half of them had already been demolished and lay in crumbled heaps of wood and plaster. Cord poked his head into each room, but there was nothing to see. When he came to another set of narrow stairs, he decided to leave.

He stiffened at the sudden feel of pressure against his lower back, as if someone were pushing him. He jerked around, but no one was there. Feeling foolish, he made a complete circle, anyway. He muttered a curse, and then eyed the stairway. Hell, he'd come this far.

The planks of wood creaked under his weight, although he felt confident that they'd hold him. When he got to the top, the door was stuck, but a firm shove with his good shoulder forced it open. Like the stairs, the entryway was narrow and he had to angle his body sideways to gain access. Ducking his head, he stepped into the small attic.

Enough light filtered in through a cloudy windowpane that he was able to find a string hanging from a bare bulb, which quickly lit the room. Unlike the rest of the house, the contents appeared to have been untouched. In the corner was a dress form next to a bolt of lacy fabric leaning against the wall. Across the room stood a full-length mirror, and behind it an old oak dresser with two missing knobs.

Dust coated everything as if untouched by human hands for some time, which didn't make sense since the rest of the house had been cleared of furniture. He thought about opening the small window but there was no use staying in the stuffy room. Nothing of interest here...

He saw the chest.

Sitting by itself on the far side of the room, it appeared free of dust. Frowning, he moved closer, and saw that it was old but in good shape. He crouched down, hoping he wouldn't have to break the lock, and discovered it unlatched. He lifted the lid and found a pair of vintage toys, hand-carved from the looks of the train pieces. There was a book, too, which he set aside, and a photo album, which he balanced on his knee and flipped open. He was curious because the album didn't seem as worn as the other things in the attic, though the photos encased in brittle plastic sheets were old and faded, mostly featuring landscapes. When he came to the one of the blonde, he angled the photo toward the light, peering closer.

Had to be a Winslow. The woman was a dead ringer for one of the missing sisters, except she wore an old-fashioned dress and her hair was longer and pinned up. His gaze skimmed the next picture and his heart thudded. The same blond woman stood with her arm linked with another woman.

Who looked exactly like the other missing sister.

He dropped the album as if it had scorched him. The photos fell free of the plastic sleeve. He picked them up. On the back was written 1877. Was this some kind of joke? Puzzled, he tucked the photos into his breast pocket just as a flash of light came from the chest. He blinked and ducked his head to find the source. All he saw was an antique camera. He picked up the big, bulky contraption, which couldn't possibly work....

Beneath his feet the floor shook violently. Shit. Nothing terrified him like an earthquake. He'd been through two of them in L.A. Hot white light flashed in his face, blinding him. With an unholy force, the earth shook again, and he flung the camera, panic clogging his throat. Trying to focus, he dropped to his knees. He had to get out. Find the door. He flailed blindly as the floor rumbled and threatened to swallow him whole.

The violence stopped as suddenly as it had begun. He stayed frozen, waiting for the aftershock. Nothing happened as his vision slowly cleared. He should have felt relief. Except he was no longer in the attic.

3

CORD SQUINTED UP at the clear blue sky. A pair of hawks circled overhead. Clouds hovered close to hills blanketed with fallen yellow and orange leaves.

He blinked blearily. Nothing changed.

He spun around. The Winslow house. It was gone. There were no buildings, only an endless dirt road and skeletal trees, their limbs forking the sky.

How was this possible? He'd been in the attic only a moment ago….

Sniffing the air, he knew he wasn't imagining the aroma of smoked meat mingled with charred hickory. That meant he was still alive, right? He looked down at his jeans and the tops of his cowboy boots, and then touched his gun through his cashmere sport jacket. The .38 caliber sat snugly in his shoulder holster.

He suddenly remembered the earthquake. The flash. The blinding white light. A gunshot? He opened his jacket and checked his blue striped cotton shirt. No blood. Only nervous sweat coated his skin. Hell. That didn't mean he wasn't dead. What other reason was there for him unexpectedly standing in the middle of nowhere?

Shading his eyes, he strained to see down both sides of the dirt road. He saw nothing, though the scent of the roasting meat seemed to have grown stronger so he had to be close to some sort of civilization. Like icy fingers squeezing the life-blood from him, a chill gripped him, and he turned up his blazer collar as he started in the direction of the tantalizing aroma. That was another thing—if he were dead, the smell wouldn't be so appealing.

He swallowed hard, but had to work at gathering enough saliva in his parched mouth. The dust he kicked up as he trudged on didn't help, so he crooked his arm over his mouth and nose. After about a quarter of a mile, he stopped and listened. He thought he heard voices. Children laughing? At least he was going in the right direction.

The thought had barely flitted through his mind when he saw the eagle. As if beckoning him, the majestic bird dipped lower in the sky before soaring back up and glided just ahead of Cord. A sure sign that he was going in the right direction.

MAGGIE DAWSON pressed a hand to her nervous belly and then gathered her long skirt in one hand and carefully climbed down off the wagon. She prayed with all her heart that today was the day she'd hear from her sister. Mary had never been the fastest letter writer but once she learned of Maggie's predicament, surely she'd responded hastily.

"Afternoon, Maggie, fine fall day we're having."

Maggie forced a polite smile on her face as she turned toward Mrs. Weaver's voice. "Yes, nice and cool. Good baking weather. I have a mind to bake a couple of apple pies for Pa. You know how he does so love his sweets."

Mrs. Weaver stopped in the middle of the boardwalk and tilted her narrow face to the side. "Come to think of it, I haven't seen him in a good long while. How's he coming along?"

Gritting her teeth, Maggie turned back to tethering her horse so Mrs. Weaver wouldn't see the bright red spots that heated Maggie's cheeks. When was she going to learn? Mrs.

Weaver would have kept on walking if Maggie hadn't opened her big mouth and rambled, and then she wouldn't have to tell a big fat lie. Which plainly she was very bad at doing, partly in thanks to her cursed fair skin and disgusting red hair.

"He's still feeling poorly. That's why I've been the one coming to town lately." Maggie cinched the reins and forced herself to face Mrs. Weaver.

"Well, honey, I wouldn't be making him apple pie if I were you. He needs a good brothy soup. Just this morning I told Harold we need to slaughter one of the chickens. I could bring some—"

"Oh, thank you, anyway, Mrs. Weaver. But I just made a pot myself this morning. Pa's probably eating some of it right now. He—" Shut up, Maggie, she told herself sternly and stepped up onto the boardwalk. She'd been lying and evading so much lately she should be better at it by now. "Say hello to Mr. Weaver for me," Maggie said as she rudely backed away from the older woman's disapproving face.

Her stomach in a twisted knot, Maggie entered Arnold's general store and went straight to the threads. She would have much rather run straight to the corner where Mr. Carlson sat at a wobbly scarred oak table and sorted and dispensed the mail, but she never wanted to appear too eager and always first bought a few yards of fabric or a new color thread that she didn't need.

After making her selection and quickly paying for her purchase, she approached Mr. Carlson with a bright smile on her face.

He looked up and smiled back. "Lordy, Miss Maggie, I do believe you have an extra sense about when the mailbag arrives. You're pert' near my first customer each week."

Her smile faltered, and she shrugged a shoulder. "Being as I'm in town, anyway…"

Over his wire-rimmed spectacles, he eyed her speculatively for a moment, and then bent his balding head to sift through a pile of letters. "Nope. Nothin' this week. You got somethin' goin' out?"

She pressed her lips together to hide her disappointment, and shook her head. "Not this time, Mr. Carlson. Thank you."

What was the use? She'd already sent Mary three letters just in case she hadn't received the first two. Maggie just had to be patient was all. Not one of her finer qualities, as Pa had reminded her often enough. Not unkindly, but just as it was a father's duty. At least he hadn't blamed that particular defect of character on the fact that at twenty-five she was a hopeless spinster. No, there were plenty of other reasons for her lack of suitors.

"Maggie?"

She'd made it to the display of mason jars next to the iron skillets, and turned back to Mr. Carlson.

"How's your pa? Ain't seen him in over two months," Mr. Carlson asked, his kind ruddy face nearly her undoing.

Maggie pressed a hand to her waist and swallowed around the lump of grief in her throat. "He's been feeling a mite poorly."

"Again?" The man frowned. "Seems he's been sick since September. Maybe you ought to have the new doc go out to your place and have a look—"

"No," she said too abruptly and forced a brittle laugh. "He hasn't been sick this whole time. He's been busy prospecting the past month. Last night it seems he ate something that didn't sit well in his belly, is all."

"Ah." Mr. Carlson smiled, clearly appeased. "Well, you take care driving that wagon home. You might tell him I noticed that left rear wheel might be wobbling some."

"I'll be sure to do that, Mr. Carlson. Thank you." Maggie hurried out of the general store before anyone else could ask her about Pa. Lord, she didn't need the wagon wheel to break now. Who'd fix the darn thing? Not Pa. Not buried twenty yards behind their cabin.

At the thought, her breath caught on a sob and she nearly stumbled off the boardwalk and into Bertha. The gray mare turned accusing eyes on Maggie, as if she knew that Maggie hadn't even dug her father a proper grave. Rock-hard ground and trembling hands had allowed for a four-foot hole and she hadn't dared wait longer to get him in the freezing ground.

God, please, please, don't let anyone find out he's gone before I hear from Mary.

How many times had she uttered the prayer but to no use? She supposed she could write her younger sister, but Clara lived with her husband and two children clear across the country somewhere outside of Boston. No, Mary was closer in San Francisco and still Maggie's best choice. As soon as her older sister received her letter she and her husband would come for her. Mary was the smart one, the brave one. She'd know exactly what to do.

Maggie unhitched Bertha, gathered her skirt with one hand and climbed onto the wagon. Seeming unfriendly or not, she kept her face straight ahead, not wishing to engage in conversation with anyone as she slowly rode out of town. If anyone knew she was staying at the cabin alone, tongues would wag. And it might not matter that Maggie had regrettable curly red hair or was taller than most of the men in Deadwood, if the miners got wind that she was a woman living alone….

Well, she wasn't precisely sure what might happen if they came sniffing around, she only knew it would be a bad thing because Pa had told her that some men simply didn't know how to treat a lady. She knew about kissing, of course, because when she was fifteen and hadn't yet sprung up that extra six inches, Clem Browning had kissed her on the mouth twice.

She and Clem had been behind the rotting barn where the whole family had lived in Kansas before Pa took it in mind to come prospecting.

As soon as she passed the smokehouse and livery at the edge of town, she breathed a sigh of relief. She took a final look over her shoulder and then clucked her tongue, signaling Bertha to pick up the pace. The fat old mare barely minded but Maggie was so grateful to be out of sight that she didn't care. A brisk wind had picked up and she pulled her wool shawl tighter around her shoulders.

Her mind was on the growing chill in the air and the dwindling woodpile behind the small two-room cabin she and Pa had shared when she saw movement in the trees to the right. She didn't slow down but kept her gaze on the scrub oak. A white-tailed doe leaped into sight before scurrying deeper into the woods.

Maggie smiled at herself and then flicked the reins, anxious suddenly to be home, snug in her little cabin. She still had laundry to do and peaches to…

He jumped in front of the wagon from out of nowhere, blocking Bertha's path with his big body. "Lady, don't scream. I just need to talk to you."

A strangled cry lodged in her throat. She yanked on the reins when she should have urged the mare to gallop. No need to panic, she told herself, not sure if her throat would work. She wasn't too terribly far from town, and the stranger said he just wanted to talk. "Wh-what do you want?"

His hair was long and as black as a moonless night. Even before she shaded her eyes from the sun she saw that he had a strong face with high broad cheekbones, a long narrow nose and a stubbornly square jaw. She squinted at the stranger, and without thinking, leaned toward him for a closer look and met dark probing eyes. She jerked back.

The saints preserve her, he was part Indian. Fear threatening to choke her, she did something she never before thought of doing. She grabbed the whip and made to use it. "Giddyap, Bertha, giddyap!"

"That's not necessary." The man shot his arm in the air and grimaced when the whip snapped across his wrist instead of poor Bertha's rump. "I'm not going to hurt you."

"Step aside, mister. Or I'll—I'll—" She swallowed hard. "Step aside. Please."

While holding on to the harness, he worked his way around Bertha and toward Maggie. "I just want to ask you a question," he said in calm, perfect English. Of course he plainly wasn't full-blooded Indian. Maybe one of those half-breeds she knew passed through Deadwood from time to time, but hadn't actually seen. He dressed funny, too. Like he might come from back east.

"What do you want to know?" she asked, surprised her voice hadn't cracked. She kept a firm grip on the whip, fervently hoping she wouldn't have to use it on him. The next time she came into town she was bringing Pa's shotgun, or even better the Spencer carbine, which she could handle easier. She was alone now, she had to consider such things.

"Where are we?" The man's gaze stayed locked on hers, while his long lean fingers stroked Bertha's flank.

She frowned at the odd question and made a motion with her chin toward town. "Deadwood."

"Deadwood," he repeated, confusion flickering in his eyes. They weren't as dark as she'd first thought, more hazel with gold and green flecks. "Where are the houses?"

"Mostly in town. There are a few cabins scattered closer to the river like—" She bit down hard on her lower lip. He didn't need to know where she lived.

The faraway look in his eyes disappeared and he focused sharply on her. "Which way is the highway?"

"The what?"

"What about the old Winslow house? It should be right…"
He shook his head and briefly closed his eyes, gripping the
side of the wagon as if to steady himself. "There was an earthquake a few minutes ago."

Maggie glanced over her shoulder toward town. Maybe the
man was sick. Should she get help? "Sometimes when they
blast at the mines the ground shakes a bit but not today. They
haven't been—"

He frowned at her. "The mines?"

"The gold mines."

"They don't still have working mines near here."

She stared at him, wondering if he were a mite touched in
the head. "That's pretty much all there is, mister."

He seemed confused, his gaze first meeting hers, and then
narrowing on the rickety old wagon. When he finally looked
back at her, their eyes met only briefly before his gaze
wandered down the front of her plain blue cotton dress, lingering long enough on her breasts that she shrunk back.

"What day it is?" he asked suddenly, his voice strained
and hoarse.

"Tuesday."

"The date," he said tersely enough to send a fresh frisson
of fear up her spine.

"November tenth or eleventh, I'm not sure."

"And the year?"

Maggie moistened her parched lips. The man was clearly
loco. She should scream. If she did, loud enough, maybe, just
maybe, someone in the livery could hear her. "Eighteen
seventy-eight."

CORD STARED NUMBLY at the woman. No teasing glint lit her
green eyes. In fact, the emerald color had darkened with fear

when he'd demanded to know the date. Her face was pale with alarm, except for the scattering of freckles across her nose, and her full lower lip quivered slightly. She looked as if she'd run if he let her. No, she wasn't teasing him. This was no hoax.

Finally, she lifted her small pointed chin. "I'll thank you to release my horse, sir. I best be on my way before my pa starts searching for me. He would not take kindly to me speaking with a stranger."

Cord stared past her in the direction from where she'd come. He'd seen the old buildings, although he'd stopped short of getting too close, and still he hadn't believed his own eyes. The place looked like any one of a dozen movie sets he'd worked on as a stuntman. But even from the outskirts, the stench of horse manure mixed with smoking meat and human waste was real. Brutally real. Goose bumps raised from his skin.

What did this mean? After the ridicule Masi and the elders indulged from him and Bobby, had they been right all along? Was this some kind of life after death he was experiencing? Had he been transported back one hundred and thirty years? But he didn't recall dying. Wouldn't he remember being shot or crushed by an earthquake?

"He always carries his shotgun with him. I should not like to see you hurt."

The woman's words barely penetrated the fog of disbelief and panic that shrouded him. "A shotgun?" He glanced down at his shirt again. Still no blood. "What shotgun?"

"My pa." She shoved away a stubborn curl of auburn hair that corkscrewed over one eye, and peered warily at him. "He carries a shotgun," she murmured, gesturing pointedly at his restraining hand. "I should like to leave now before he comes to fetch me."

He started to release the harness, but then again checked

the direction in which she was traveling. Better he take his chances of finding out what the hell was going on from her folks than from a town full of nosy people who'd have more questions than he could answer. "Is that where you're headed? Away from town?"

Her pink lips parted for a long silent moment, the pulse at the side of her slender neck leaping wildly. "Pardon me?"

"Your home…is it that way?"

"Why?"

"I'd like a word with your father."

"My—? No. You can't." She shook her head, her lips drawing into a thin line. "No. You can't."

Cord growled in frustration. "Look, lady. I don't have much of a choice." Anger laced with fear flashed in her eyes. Even the mare sensed the tension and whinnied. Made him realize that because of his own panic, he was going about this all wrong. "My name is Cord," he said, and soothingly stroked the side of the mare's neck. "Cord Braddock. What's your name?"

She hesitated. "Maggie." Her throat worked as she swallowed. "Maggie Dawson." Her gaze darted to the hand he'd slowly moved toward the reins. When she sensed what he was about to do, she jerked the reins to the side and used them to slap the mare's broad rump.

"Giddyap, Bertha!" she cried desperately but the old mare barely moved. "Giddyap."

"Can't let you do that, Maggie Dawson," he said as he jumped up on the seat beside her, causing the whole wagon to list heavily to one side.

She fell against him, blushing furiously, and then quickly righted herself. "What are you doing?"

"I'm not going to hurt you. I just need some answers."

"You have to get off. Right now." She edged over as far away from him as possible. "Go."

Cord sighed wearily. "How far is it?"

"I'm not taking you anywhere."

"Yes, you are."

"I'll scream. I swear I will."

"I'm sorry about this, Maggie," Cord said as he reached under his jacket for the .38. "I truly am. But you will take me home."

4

MAGGIE'S EYES widened at the small gun he showed her, her fascination with its diminutive size and the contraption holding it inside his jacket momentarily replacing her fear. The brown leather straps were some kind of holster, except that she'd never seen one fit over a man's shoulder before. That didn't seem terribly practical. Not for speed, anyway. Irrationally the idea helped calm her.

"I really don't want to hurt you," the man repeated, reaching for the gun. "But I will if you scream."

The fear rushed back. She tamped down the desire to jump off the wagon and run toward town. But what chance would she have if he truly meant to do her harm? Instead, she raised her gaze to his. "What do you want?"

"I'm a detective. I'm looking for two missing women." He withdrew his hand, leaving the gun inside his jacket, his eyes sharp and alert as he assessed her face.

"Are you a Pinkerton?"

He hesitated, not a reassuring sign. "Something like that."

"I didn't know they hired Indians," Maggie murmured thoughtlessly, immediately regretting her words. His face darkened, and she averted her gaze, her heart starting to pound harder. The truth was, she didn't know much about the private security agency at all, except for gossip she'd heard about some of their agents having proved untrustworthy. "You should talk to the sheriff."

"I'm not ready to do that yet." The stranger surprised her by releasing the reins to her. "Let's go."

She took a deep breath and tried not to focus where his coat gapped, allowing for a glimpse of the odd-looking gun. There was little to do but comply with his demand and pray he didn't hurt her. If she gave Bertha her head, the lazy mare would lumber at a snail's pace and Maggie might get lucky and someone would happen by before they reached the fork that would take them to her cabin. Once they got there, she had no idea what she would do when he found out she lived alone.

The thought made her shudder violently and she nearly lost control of the reins. The man turned toward her but she kept facing forward, then she straightened her spine. As soon as they got to the cabin, she had to get to the rifle leaning on the wall behind the door before he saw it. She'd have the upper hand then. She'd simply make him go away. Threaten to put a hole in him the size of Texas.

God help her, could she actually kill a man? She shuddered again.

"Maggie?"

She jumped. Not just at his familiarity, but at the warm breath that danced across her cheek and stirred the stubborn curls that had escaped the bun at her nape. She moved her shoulder because his were so broad that he kept brushing against her arm.

Drawing her shawl tighter, she moistened her dry lips. "Yes?"

He gently, briefly touched the back of her wrist. "You should be wearing gloves."

She blinked at him, and then at the patch of skin where he'd pressed the tips of his long lean fingers. Her flesh burned— no, tingled was more like it—where he'd touched her. She wanted to rub away the odd sensation, but she only stared at the unsightly red gash that wound around her pale knuckles.

There were calluses, too, on the pads of her thumbs and on the one finger where she'd once dreamed a ring would've been placed years ago.

How scratched and ugly her hands were from tending the garden and carrying wood to the stove, from scrubbing clothes and the cabin's wood floors. Not at all like a proper lady's hands ought to look. Even when Pa had been alive, he'd sometimes be out prospecting for days on end and the chores had to get done somehow. She'd always worked hard and she wasn't ashamed of that.

Fisting her hands, she wanted to hide them suddenly, away from his prying eyes. Instead, she lifted her chin and said nothing. Whether she wore gloves or not was none of his concern. He'd be better off worrying how he'd get back to town once she got her hands on Pa's Spencer carbine rifle.

Her rifle now.

The words echoed tauntingly in her head. She bit down on her lower lip until the coppery taste of blood touched her tongue. It was only her now. Only her.

Without thinking, she glanced over her shoulder. The barren dirt road wound back toward Deadwood. They were nearing the fork that would take them along the creek and to her cabin.

He followed her gaze, his eyes coming gravely back to meet hers. "Let's step it up."

He talked funny, dressed funny and smelled too good for a man. Pretty fancy, in fact, for an Indian. Was he really a Pinkerton? Could it be that he simply was looking for two missing women? But why not contact the sheriff?

She cleared her throat. "Who are they? The women you're looking for?"

"Two sisters. Reese and Ellie Winslow. One blonde, one brunette," he said absently, his apparent preoccupation worrying her.

She squinted against the setting sun filtering through the trees and wondered why he wasn't more interested if he really had been hired to find them. "And you think they're in Deadwood?"

"I don't know."

At his impatient tone, she slid him a sidelong glance. His gaze scanned the tall prairie grass and scrub brush close to the road and then darted out to where the ponderosa pines started their climb uphill.

She tried not to think about what was sure to happen once they reached the cabin in the next twenty minutes. And then she realized that a plan was exactly what she should be thinking about. She'd have to act fast to get to the gun first and bring it up high enough to do any good. If they tussled over it, she'd lose. That simple. He was too tall and broad, and…

She slid another look his way. His left shoulder stood a good six inches above hers, and to her utter amazement, a thrill coursed through her. Even Pa had been shorter than she was, and both Mary and Clara certainly, by nearly a foot. Her gaze went to his big hands and long lean fingers. How easily he could choke the life out of her. The sobering thought made her recall what had to be done and it didn't seem long before the small cabin came into view.

They'd had almost no money with them when they'd come west so the place wasn't much. But her pa had been good with a hammer so the cabin's roof no longer leaked, and one side of the sagging red barn where they kept their milk cow, a few chickens and Bertha stayed dry most of the time.

On the left, closer to the creek, sat Maggie's pride and joy. The square of garden not only helped keep them fed for a good part of the year, but she'd also lovingly planted an assortment of colorful flowers that she sometimes snipped and brought into the house to sit in a canning jar in the kitchen. The air had been too cold lately and the flowers were gone now. Just like Pa.

She briefly squeezed her eyes shut. God help her, she had to stop thinking about him. At least for now.

"This is it?" the man asked slowly.

She wished she could remember his name. Although in a few more minutes it wouldn't matter. Either way. She swallowed hard and nodded, but he wasn't looking at her. She replied, "Yes. This is where *we* live."

"Who else besides you and your father?"

She took a moment too long to answer and sighed. What would be the use of lying further? "That's all."

He took the reins from her. "Where is he?"

"Either inside or washing up at the creek." She started to climb down, but he touched her arm.

"Stay where you are." As if he didn't trust her, he kept hold of the reins as he jumped down from the wagon. It didn't matter. Bertha hadn't even waited for a cue but plodded slowly toward the barn in search of grain. The man jerked on the reins. "Where the hell is she going?"

"She's thirsty and she wants to be fed, and there is certainly no need for that kind of language." Using the opportunity for Bertha's abrupt stop, Maggie carefully climbed down. "I'll need to unhitch her and get her watered."

The stranger looked unconvinced and then motioned with his chin. He followed so close behind that Maggie knew then that when the time came, it wouldn't be easy getting to the rifle first. Her only advantage was that she alone knew where it lay hidden. She tried to still her trembling hands as she worked to release Bertha from the traces. He came up behind her suddenly, his chest rubbing against her back, and she jumped so hard that her head thwacked his chin.

"Christ, I was just trying to help." He jerked away, soothing the offended area, and only then did she notice he was trying to lift the harness for her.

"Sorry," she murmured, still feeling the heat where their bodies had met. "But I'd thank you kindly not to take the Lord's name in vain."

"What?" He bit out the word, and then his face relaxed. "It's just an expression. It doesn't mean anything."

"It does to me." She turned away and finished tending Bertha.

"Why hasn't your father come out? Shouldn't he have heard us?"

"Apparently not," she said crisply.

He sighed and stepped a good distance away. "Look, I'm sorry. I'll try to watch my language."

She gave a small nod, her thoughts swirling. If he were truly a bad man, he wouldn't apologize. Or he wouldn't have tried to help her with Bertha, for that matter. Maybe when he found out that Pa wasn't around he'd just leave. Was going for the rifle right off wise on her part?

The problem was, once they were inside and the door was closed, he'd see the shooting iron. Maybe she could leave the door open, pretend she wanted to air out the room. Yes, that was the most prudent plan.

She gave Bertha a quick rubdown, silently promising to come out later and do a proper job, and then portioned some oats for the mare. That was another foreseeable problem if Mary didn't answer soon. Eventually Maggie would have to replenish feed, which meant she had to trade some gold.

"All done," she said with forced brightness as she lifted the hem of her skirt and spun toward him.

His gaze swiftly moved up to her face. Where he'd been staring she had no earthly idea. Unless she had a tear in the back of her skirt. The thought brought a surge of heat up her neck and into her cheeks, but she couldn't very well check for rips now.

He pushed off from the post he'd been leaning on and

motioned for her to precede him. Self-conscious, she walked stiffly ahead of him. Thankfully once they left the barn he stayed abreast of her all the way to the cabin.

She opened the door and for the sake of pretense called out, "Pa, I'm home." Since there were only two rooms, that's where the deception ended. She shrugged and pushed the door wide. "He must be out back."

His gaze narrowed. "Wouldn't he have heard us?"

"He could be out prospecting. I can't know where he is at every second of the day." Her eyes widened when she realized how shrewish she'd sounded. "I'm sorry. I don't know how long he'll be," she said, averting her gaze. It automatically went to the man's hand as it closed around the doorknob. "Leave that door open, please. It's stuffy in here."

"Stuffy? It's chilly." He pulled the door toward him.

"Don't." Tensing, ready to yank the knob from his hand, she met his eyes.

He looked surprised at first, then suspicious.

She tried to look relaxed, but stayed where she was in case she needed to take action. "It's not proper for us to be alone, you know that. Pa will be most upset if the door is closed when he returns."

He studied her as if trying to decide if he should trust her. But she hadn't lied. A gentleman knew it was improper for an unmarried lady to entertain him alone. Requesting that the door remain open was perfectly acceptable.

Finally he snorted and, looking around the small room, murmured under his breath, "And he'll pull out his shotgun."

Her flaming cheeks surely gave her away. Having no choice, she dove behind the door for the carbine.

THANKS TO OVER ten years of stunt work, Cord still had lightning reflexes. He grabbed her wrist just as she was about to wrap her hand around the rifle barrel. "You crazy fool. I said I wouldn't hurt you."

She struggled, twisting her hand to get free, shoving him with her other hand, but she was no match for him. Although she did get in a couple of good licks to his injured shoulder. He winced, gripping her fragile wrist tighter than he'd meant to. She gasped, her face flushed with exertion, and quit her fight.

He wasn't as quick to release her. Another jab to his throbbing shoulder and he'd want to wring her neck. He kicked the rifle out of reach, and kept her pinned to the wall. A tremor wracked her body and the fear he saw in her dark green eyes gave him pause. He loosened his grip but wasn't foolish enough to let her go.

"You said you wouldn't hurt me," she taunted softly, trying to flex her trapped wrist.

"Don't play that game with me."

She briefly averted her gaze, her breath coming out in small quick pants and tickling the skin at the V of his shirt. The woman was tall, had to be about five-ten, slender and small-boned. With that fair skin of hers, he was bound to leave bruises. None of this was her fault. Wrong place, wrong time. Shame spilled over him.

He released her, and grabbed the rifle before she could get to it. "You even know how to use this?"

"Hand it over and I'll show you." She shot him a resentful look as she rubbed the skin around her wrist.

"Sorry, but I had to defend myself."

"That's what I was going to say."

Cord smiled. "Touché."

She frowned. "I don't know what that means, mister, and I don't care. I'm asking you nicely to please leave."

"It's Cord," he said absently, studying the rifle. Not just a prop that he'd seen a hundred times, but the real deal. Beautiful workmanship. "Cord Braddock."

When he eventually looked over at her, the stark terror in her eyes sliced through him.

"I wasn't really going to shoot you," she said, shrinking back to press her spine against the door's hinges.

He realized his fascination with the Spencer carbine had frightened her. Lowering the rifle to his side, he automatically reached out his other hand to comfort her. With a whimper, she crumpled halfway to the bare plank floor.

"Maggie, no. I was just—" He withdrew his hand and shoved it through his hair. "Look, I'll unload the rifle so neither of us will think about using it. How's that?"

"I reckon that might be a fine idea," she murmured, her terrified gaze glued to the end of the barrel.

He stared down at the stock, hoping he could figure out how to unload it since the prop guys usually took care of that kind of thing. And then the thought hit. He looked up at her. "It's not loaded."

"Oh." Slowly she inched back up the wall. "You still have that small gun. Is it loaded?"

"Yes."

"Maybe you should—"

"No." He leaned the rifle back against the rough wood wall. No way would he unload the sucker and leave himself that vulnerable. He still had no idea where the hell he was.

1878 Deadwood.

How was that possible? His gaze took in the woman's plain long-sleeve blue dress, buttons down the entire bodice, clunky black shoes, the gray wool shawl that had fallen to the plank floor. All of it straight out of a Hollywood studio's costume closet. Even the way she wore her hair, pulled back in a tight bun at her nape, made her look the part of an old-fashioned spinster. Or would have if her unruly auburn hair had cooperated. Instead, tendrils curled around her face and clung to the side of her neck, giving her the kind of sexy tousled look that hairstylists on movie sets spent hours trying to create.

She visibly swallowed, pressing a hand to her midsection, and he guessed he'd stared too long. The last thing he wanted to do was frighten her further.

"I thought I'd put a couple of logs on the fire and make some coffee," she said in a small voice. "If that's all right."

"Sure." He waved a hand, and she hurried toward the pile of wood stacked next to the stove. The door was still open and it was cool in the cabin. He thought about closing the door, since he'd figured out the reason for leaving it open was to hide the rifle, but then again, if she felt more comfortable with it open until her father returned, that was okay with Cord.

He made sure she was out of striking distance and then peered through the window framed by blue checked curtains. He could see the sagging barn and the corral next to it where a chestnut grazed. Probably her father's horse. The animal was in much better shape than the mare she used to pull the wagon.

"How many horses do you have?" he asked over his shoulder.

"Well, there's Bertha, of course. She pulls the wagon. And then there's Red, a chestnut we bought from a driver last year. Red's Pa's horse." Her voice caught, and she quickly turned away to light a lamp.

Cord continued to stare out the window. If the chestnut was here, her father had to be nearby. Apparently she'd just worked that out for herself and didn't want to alert Cord. He spotted a well halfway between the cabin and what appeared to be a shed. The small structure was barely big enough to hold a...

"Shit." An outhouse?

He looked over just as her lips thinned into a disapproving line. He didn't bother to apologize this time, although he would try to watch himself. But given the circumstances, if she'd suddenly been dropped into his world, the prim Ms. Dawson would probably be cussing, too.

After a final glance around the outside perimeter, he turned back to watch her measure out coffee grounds. Everything seemed surreal. The heavy iron kettle, the potbellied stove, even the plain oak kitchen table that no one had bothered to finish properly. Yet there were small decorative touches like the blue-and-white runner that ran down the middle of the table and the braided rug near the door that matched the blue gingham curtains. A glass jar of dried flowers sat near a metal washbasin.

Cord frowned. Near the same basin sat one cup and one plate and one fork. Odd, or was he reading too much into it? Her father could have left them behind after he'd finished his lunch. Or there was no father. Around here, a man wouldn't leave an unloaded rifle at the ready. His gaze drew to the semi-open door to the only other room in the cabin. A bedroom?

He turned toward Maggie and found her nervously watching him. She looked away and dragged her palms down a beige apron she'd tied around her waist.

"I need to get some water," she said, reaching for a metal bucket. "Then I'll make the coffee."

"Where do you get the water from?"

She wrinkled her nose at him as if she thought him dimwitted. "The well."

"Ah, of course." Not dimwitted, just freakin' nuts. He needed time to sort this out. Review the events of the day. Maybe this whole thing had something to do with the camera flash. But what? Had Masi had a hand in this? God, he hated that his mind kept going back to the old Navajo legends. They were just stories told by the Dine. Just silly stories.

"So I'll be right back." She'd made it to the door before he registered she'd even moved.

"I'll get it."

"That's not necessary," she said hastily.

"Better yet, we'll go together."

Her face fell. "You really should think about going to town. It'll be dark before long."

"Don't worry about me, Maggie." He smiled and took the bucket from her. "I figure I'll be spending the night."

5

MAGGIE JERKED so hard, the bucket flung wildly toward her. "You can't stay here."

Cord smiled and again took the bucket from her. "That's not very hospitable being as I'm your guest."

"My guest?" She stared at the way his mouth quirked at the corners. Was he teasing her? She used the back of her wrist to push the hair away from her face. "You've forced yourself in here, Mr. Braddock. That hardly qualifies you as a welcome guest."

"Let's see what your father says, shall we?" He stepped aside and gestured her out the front door.

With a brusque swirl of her skirt, she passed him. "He's going to be angry, I can assure you of that right now. And he has a temper, a very, very bad temper. Especially if he's been drinking, which is what he might be doing at this very minute."

"Thanks for the warning."

"He's good with a gun, too. Fast with perfect aim."

"Even when he's drinking, huh?"

She sniffed when she heard the smile in his voice, as if he knew she was lying her head off. "Sometimes if he gets too drunk, the sheriff or the deputy escorts him home. They come inside for coffee before they head back to town."

"Good to know. That would save me a trip."

Maggie gritted her teeth and said no more until they got to

the well. With false bravery, she said, "I'll make beans for supper. There's some leftover cornbread. After you eat, you can bed down in the barn."

When he didn't respond, she snuck a peek at him as she reached for the pulley rope above the well. He was looking around, his eyes alert to the dusky shadows beginning to fall over the tall grass beyond the clearing. At this time of year sunset seemed like a circus magic act. Bright one moment and then sinking fast at the end, leaving behind pink wispy clouds against a gray sky.

In the distance, a coyote howled and, hating the eerie sound, Maggie quickly hauled up the bucket of water. The rope cut into her work-roughened hands and it riled her that she suddenly cared about the scars and calluses that marred her palms.

"Here." With one hand, Cord lifted the heavy bucket from her and dumped the water into the pail.

She saw him wince and then briefly probe his right shoulder, before returning the bucket to its place above the well and then picking up the full pail with his other hand. She turned back toward the cabin, and they walked in silence until they got near the front door. "After I put the beans on I have chores to do out here," she said, and then added quickly, "Pa usually does them but if he's not back before sundown I take care of the horses and the chickens."

"What's he riding?" Cord gestured toward Red. "If the chestnut is his."

"A mustang he recently broke and means to sell at auction." Her quickness surprised even her. She was going straight to hell for all the easy lies. If Mary didn't get here soon there would be no hope for her eternal soul.

The corners of his mouth lifted slightly. "Okay, when you're done in the kitchen, I'll help you out here."

Maggie's heart fell. "That isn't necessary," she muttered,

going ahead of him through the front door. "I know your shoulder is hurt."

She wasn't prepared for the firm grip on her arm before he roughly spun her around to face him. Water sloshed out of the pail onto the floor and on her boots.

"How do you know that?" he asked tersely, setting down the pail and taking a step toward her.

She shrunk back, her heel catching on a loose plank she'd meant to fix. He was big and broad, his face dark and threatening, and her mouth went so dry it felt as if her tongue had swelled. "I saw you favor it," she managed to say in a voice she almost didn't recognize.

Dark brows knitted together as if she were speaking some strange language that he needed to interpret, and then something passed through his eyes that looked like relief. His features relaxed and he stooped to reclaim the pail. "You want this in the kitchen?"

She nodded, not trusting herself to speak. After waiting until the way was clear, she moved widely around him to get to the sideboard, where she kept her best cast-iron pot. Quickly she got the coffee started and then the beans on, thought briefly about adding some bacon, and decided she didn't want to feed him that well. In fact, she hoped the cornbread had dried out since last night's supper. But she'd wrapped it well in a clean cloth and had churned fresh butter this morning because that's all she'd planned on fixing for herself tonight.

For over two months now she'd lived in dread that someone would come to the cabin and find out her pa was dead. Only Lester, the deputy, had come knocking and both times he'd shown up she'd managed to convince him that Pa was out prospecting. Now, what she wouldn't give for the deputy—or anyone—to come calling, even that nosy Mrs. Weaver.

She angled a brief peek at him sitting at the table, where he'd hunkered down after throwing another log on the fire. He stared out the window a lot but he still seemed to follow her every move. Clara had once claimed that she read that Indians had special tracking powers, almost like having eyes in the back of their heads. But Clara was often prone to whimsy, lived with her head in the clouds most of the time, Pa liked to say.

Maggie blinked away a tear. She missed her family. Although she couldn't dwell on them right now; she had to keep her mind clear. Swallowing a lump of emotion, she took a deep breath as she stirred the beans.

Goodness, it just occurred to her that if anyone did happen by, and they found her alone with a man—not just a man but an Indian—she'd be ruined. Her reputation would never survive the scandal. She'd even heard of white women who had killed themselves rather than be taken by a savage. What was the term? Blessed release? Shuddering, Maggie studied him discretely. He wasn't exactly a savage. A half-breed who dressed better and was cleaner than most men in Deadwood, for sure. But that wouldn't matter to the menfolk around here. She'd be branded for life.

As if he'd felt the weight of her stare, he turned to meet her eyes. It frightened her that she couldn't read his impassive face. He'd claimed he didn't mean to harm her. Did he have any idea of the predicament he'd placed her in? Did he care? The real question she needed to ask herself was…was it better to be ruined or dead?

SMELLING THE beans simmer, Cord's stomach rumbled. That he could think about food at all was laughable. That is, if he weren't so damned confused. And angry. And, worst, fear had left a bitter taste on his tongue.

He didn't understand any of this, which meant he didn't know how to solve the problem. Overwhelming helplessness pressed heavily against his chest, making it hard to even breathe. It had been eighteen years since he'd last felt so powerless, the day he'd left the reservation.

Another whiff of beans teased his nostrils and the reason hit him why he could be relaxed enough to feel hunger. Beans and rice and fried bread had been staples for him and Masi. When the tourist season died down, or her beadwork hadn't sold well and money was low, they'd lived on nothing else for weeks. He'd sworn when he left the reservation he'd never touch the stuff again. And he hadn't. At least not after he'd started making some serious money. But now, the savory smell comforted him, lulled him into remembering simpler times spent with Masi.

Until he looked into the auburn-haired woman's accusing eyes. He wasn't just a man keeping her trapped, but he was an Indian. For her, for so many others, that was crime enough. Not that her racist attitude excused him for one second. He knew he was scum and he wished he had thought beyond taking this coward's way to buy some time, but it was too late. He was in too deep. She could finger him, and the best he could hope for would be a cot in the local jail, and at worst, a noose around his neck.

Especially if this really was 1878.

The more he looked around the small room, at the primitive stove, the cookware, the lack of plumbing, at the woman herself wearing a homemade dress worn at the cuffs and elbows, the more convinced he was becoming that he'd somehow slipped through a time warp. Crazy, yeah, but even though he wasn't the sharpest P.I. in Hollywood, he knew evidence when he saw it.

His gaze snagged on what looked like a pamphlet sitting under some sewing supplies, and he swept the pincushion and a spool of thread aside so he could read the top. It was an 1877 Montgomery Ward catalog.

Stunned, he muttered something out loud, not sure what, but it got Maggie's attention. She hurried to the table in a swirl of fabric and snatched the paper out of his hand.

"Don't touch that. It's my only copy." She folded it in fourths and stuck it in a pocket secreted by the folds of her voluminous dress.

"I was just looking at the…darn thing."

"I suppose you think it's silly, too."

"What?"

Her cheeks flushed. "That I would want a decent stove or one of those brand-new washing machines."

"Not me," he said.

"Well, Pa thinks—" She faltered and turned away to stir the pot again. "I happen to know that Montgomery Ward has a very good reputation, even though the goods come all the way from Chicago, and that people order through the mail from them all the time."

Cord shook his head and cast his gaze back to the window. If she was lying about having a father, she was doing a good job. Half the time he was convinced it was a ruse to chase him off, and then... Come to think of it, at this point in time, a woman simply wouldn't be living by herself out here.

She turned back around and eyed him curiously. "Wouldn't surprise me none if you got your duds from a catalog. I haven't seen cloth that fine around here."

"L.A.," he said absently.

"Pardon me?"

"California."

Her eyes lit up. "San Francisco?"

He smiled. Close enough. "Yep."

She abandoned the beans, a wistful look on her face as she brought out a crock of butter and a pan wrapped in a white cloth. "I'll be going there soon. I bet they have all kinds of nice shops. A person wouldn't even need a catalog. They could go right downtown and pick out anything they wanted."

"You going there with your father?"

Her face pinched into a brief frown before she turned away again. "My sister Mary lives there."

"They have more than nice shops. You ever seen the ocean, Maggie?"

She shook her head and slowly looked at him.

"So big and blue, stretches as far as the eye can see. Makes you think anything is possible." He recalled suddenly how Masi used to utter that same phrase as they sat and watched an unusually beautiful sunset together, or had happened upon a spotted fawn being born in the tall grass.

A smile tugged at Maggie's lips. "I've seen pictures. But I'd like very much to see the ocean for myself." Once she gave in to the smile, her face transformed. Her eyes sparkled and the pink tinge of excitement in her cheeks caught him off guard. She was actually very pretty.

Pictures.

Immediately the word echoed in his brain like a sound bouncing off canyon walls.

How could he have forgotten? His gaze ran down Maggie's old-fashioned dress to her high-top shoes, and he drew back his jacket and reached into the pocket. What if the same thing that happened to him had happened to the Winslow sisters? It was a long shot, or maybe not, considering how they were dressed in the photos.

"I want to show you something," he said, getting to his feet.

Maggie scurried backward until she was stopped by the shelving where she kept her pots. The smile was gone from her face, her skin suddenly so pale her freckles stood out. Her gaze was leveled on his chest.

Bewildered, he slowly withdrew the photographs and

looked to see what had suddenly frightened her. The gun. He sighed. As much as he hated her jumping every time she caught a glimpse of it, he wasn't disarming himself.

"I just want to show you these pictures," he said quietly. "They're of the two missing women."

She put a shaky hand to her throat, briefly closed her eyes and nodded. They each took a couple of tentative steps toward the other. She stopped first and held out her hand for the photos. He passed them to her, and noticed what great pain she took trying to keep from brushing his fingers. Maybe she thought touching an Indian would somehow be infectious.

He swiftly pushed aside the unbidden thought. Being sensitive over old wounds wasn't going to get him anywhere.

"You recognize either of them?"

She stared hard at the grainy photo of the two women with their arms linked. "I think this one," she said slowly, pointing to Reese Winslow. "But it's hard to tell."

Cord's pulse leaped. "Look at the second picture. The one of her alone."

She went to the next photo. "Yes, the likeness is strong. She's a healer, isn't she?"

This time his heart did everything but explode from his chest. He nodded. "In her time, she's a doctor."

Maggie's puzzled gaze shot up to his. "Her time?"

God, was he seriously starting to believe that... Masi's voice cut into his thoughts. *Anything is possible.* He couldn't go there. Not now. "Was it in town where you saw her? When?"

"She was in town for a while, but I didn't actually see her with my own eyes." Maggie concentrated on the photo, worrying her lower lip. "I saw a sketch of her on Wanted posters outside the jail and the general store."

"A Wanted poster?"

She shrugged a slim shoulder and tried to return the photo. "Maybe I'm wrong."

"Take another look. Why was the woman wanted?"

She studied Reese's photo again. "She's beautiful," she said with the same wistfulness he'd seen earlier. "People said that about her, too. The ones who'd seen her...they said that she was too pretty and refined to be a—" Maggie cut herself short, her eyes as big as dinner plates when she looked up at him.

"Tell me, Maggie. I need to know everything you can tell me."

She pushed the photos back into his hands, hurried to the pot of fragrant beans and stirred furiously.

"Please. It's important." When she didn't respond, he added, "You want to get rid of me, don't you?"

The wooden spoon in her hand stopped midstir, and she turned hopeful eyes on him. "If I tell you everything I know, will you leave?"

"Possibly."

She straightened, excited anticipation starting to curve her mouth.

"But I can't promise."

Her lips thinned again.

"Just trying to be honest." Right. He knew damn well he wasn't going anywhere now that it was dark. He needed sleep and a plan before he went barreling into town with no horse or viable currency. Although as anxious as she was to get rid of him, he had a feeling Maggie would help him out in both areas.

She appeared to be considering her options and then said, "I only heard gossip, mind you, but it's been said that she saved two children. She did some other healing, too, while she worked with Doc."

"Go on. How did she end up on a Wanted poster?"

Her lips parted, but nothing came out. Abruptly, she turned back to the cloth-wrapped pan and picked it up, while noisily grabbing two bowls and spoons off the shelf. "Supper's ready."

Cord sighed with annoyance. What was she holding back? He took the pan and bowls from her.

"I'll bring the beans to the table." She grabbed a clean cloth with one hand and used her apron with the other to lift the pot from the stove. Carefully she protected the battered table with the cloth before setting down the pot. "Oh, the butter."

"I'll get it," he said, roughly setting down the pan and clattering bowls, his patience slipping. In spite of himself, his stomach rumbled when the faint smell of molasses drifted up to his nostrils.

She darted him a nervous look. "It's on the—"

He set the crock near the pan.

"We'll need a knife."

He'd already swiped it off the shelf and balanced the wooden handle over the crock. "Can we sit now?"

"Of course," she muttered, pulling out the chair across from his.

While she served the beans into the two bowls, he lowered himself carefully onto the crudely made ladder-back oak chair he'd used before, with renewed doubt that it could continue to hold his weight. Assured, he relaxed and picked up his spoon.

She stared dumbly at him, her palms pressed together.

"What?"

"We have to say grace."

"Ah, Jesus."

She got that pinched look again, and then her face softened into a pleased expression. "At least we have the same God. I thought Indians—" She promptly closed her mouth and lowered her gaze. Bowing her head, she prayed silently for a few seconds, and then without looking at him, picked up her spoon.

He sighed, telling himself it was useless to get angry. For all she knew he streaked his face with war paint, stuck feathers in his hair and took scalps when the urge struck. He couldn't fault her for the beliefs of the time. Well-founded beliefs at that. He wasn't ignorant of ancient tribal atrocities, regardless of what he thought the white man had deserved. He grunted to himself. White blood flowed through his veins as well.

After they each took their first bite, he asked, "Exactly what is it that you're so afraid to tell me about the woman?"

She sputtered, bringing a white cloth napkin to her lips.

"Not a very gentlemanly observation," she said with a lift of her chin.

He shrugged, unconcerned. "I'm listening."

Her face flushed, and then she blurted, "She was a runaway soiled dove who worked at the Golden Slipper."

Cord thought for a moment, and then snorted. "A prostitute?"

Maggie stared into her beans. "That's what it said on the Wanted poster. That and she ran away with a horse thief. Could be gossip though because as soon as the sheriff got killed, the poster came down."

Cord absently shook his head as he took the cornbread she offered and slathered the piece with butter. Hope began to crumble faster than the edges of the cornbread. The woman couldn't be Reese Winslow. "Anything else I should know?"

"You can find out more from the new sheriff. I could take you as far as the livery at the edge of town," she offered. "Bertha knows her way in the dark. It would be no trouble."

Cord chewed for several seconds, and then glanced toward the bedroom door. "First thing tomorrow. Tonight, I need rest."

As she followed his gaze, her face went white, and she made the sign of the cross.

6

MAGGIE DREW OUT her evening chores as long as possible. Bad enough she'd waited until it was too dark to go out to the barn without needing to light two lanterns, but Cord shadowed her every move. Her hands couldn't seem to stop trembling and what little she'd managed to eat at supper wasn't sitting well in her fluttering belly.

At least she'd finally forced herself to stop chattering about her pa coming home, and the man had stopped asking questions about him. Her only comforting thought was that he hadn't made any ungentlemanly move toward her. And mercy, he'd given her a small shock by helping her clean up the kitchen, then getting wood from the pile by the corral and fetching more water.

She wasn't fooled that he still kept track of her whereabouts even while he was outside. He'd insisted that the curtains and door stay open, and he was never out of sight, which meant she hadn't been able to do a proper job of washing. She wondered now that it was too late, if she shouldn't have at least tried to barricade herself in the bedroom.

"Maggie?"

She jumped at the sound of his deep rumbling voice and let the towel she'd been folding fall to the floor. After retrieving it, she turned to look at him. He'd slid off his jacket, and her gaze went straight to the gun in the odd shoulder contraption.

His mouth twisted in a wry smile. "Yes, it's going to stay loaded," he said, withdrawing it from the leather sheath. "No, I don't plan on using it." He stuck the gun into his waistband and unfastened the buckle of the holster, his mouth thinning into a grim line. "Unless I have to."

"I won't give you cause," she murmured, her fascination switching to the definition of muscle beneath the smooth fabric of his shirt. "Unless you give me cause," she added, and then clamped her mouth shut and met his gaze when she realized what she'd said.

Amusement flickered like molten gold in his eyes. "We have a deal then."

She gave a curt nod, knew it was time to look away, but her fascination with his chest held her spellbound. The finely woven fabric molded to the mounds and contours of his body, the like of which she'd never seen. Almost as if he wore some sort of padding beneath his shirt.

Granted, she hadn't been around many men. Not this close, anyway. Well, only Pa, in fact, and Clara's husband once when he'd taken off his shirt after getting splashed with mud from the stuck wagon wheel the spring before they'd headed east. But surely she would've noticed other men around town when it rained or when the crude miners came up from splashing their faces from the horse trough in front of the Silver Nugget.

He set aside the strappy holster and started unbuttoning his shirt, exposing his smooth hairless chest inch by inch with each button he slid from its hole. Maggie tried to look away. She had to, for pity's sake. It was indecent of him to undress in front of her. Twice as indecent for her to watch.

"Wh-what are you doing?" she asked, forcing her gaze to his blank face.

"Getting ready for bed."

"You're t-taking off your shirt." The words barely made it past her lips.

"It's the only one I have, sweetheart, and I'm feeling ripe enough already." He peeled the fabric back to fully expose his chest and then shrugged the shirt off the rest of the way. He sniffed the area of cloth under the arm and asked, "You got any laundry detergent?"

Heat seared Maggie's cheeks. Her knees would surely give out. He was perfect. All sinew and light brown skin. Like a bronze statue in one of those picture books she'd seen back in Missouri. Muscle, she realized with a start. He was padded by sleek, powerful muscle. It rippled across his lean belly, and mounded beneath flat brown nipples.

The saints preserve her, why wasn't she looking away? Why couldn't she force herself to turn…

"Are you going to keep staring, or get me some soap?" he snapped, his fingers trailing the scar that arced over his right shoulder.

She blinked, and stiffened. "I'm sorry."

"Yeah, I know. You never saw an Indian before."

"No," she agreed numbly, abruptly turning away, vaguely relieved he thought that was the reason she'd been so rude. Did Indian men all have bodies like that? Is that why white men hated them so? "Tomorrow is wash day."

"I can't wait. Unless you want me hanging around longer." His mocking tone was enough to bring her to her senses.

"The washing soap is outside near the tub, but it's too dark." To busy herself, she unnecessarily moved her sewing across the table. The lantern. She could take the lantern and bring the soap inside. With purpose, she headed for the lantern sitting next to the washbasin.

He cut her off, putting a hand to the small of her back as he reached around her. "No need. I'll use this."

His warm palm blistering her through the cotton of her dress and the muslin of her chemise was bad enough, but the back of her hand grazed his naked midsection and she feared she might swoon. She teetered slightly, unmercifully in his direction, and he slid an arm around her waist.

"You okay?"

"Don't touch me." She slapped his hand away, shoved mindlessly at his chest. His powerful naked chest. She whimpered as she fell against the sideboard.

He abruptly released her, confusion turning to anger and gathering like a winter storm in his eyes. He stared at her, then snatched up the soap she kept beside the basin. "Don't worry. Today's your lucky day," he said silkily. "I'm in no mood for raping or pillaging or taking scalps."

She opened her mouth to tell him her reaction had nothing to do with him being an Indian, but God help her she wasn't sure that was totally true, and she pressed her lips together rather than tell an unnecessary lie. Besides, she hadn't seen him this angry before. She gripped the edge of the sideboard, watching him pour the extra water he'd brought in earlier from the large-mouthed pitcher and fill the basin.

He then submerged the shirt before dropping in the soap. To her utter amazement, he started furiously scrubbing. Not once had Pa washed his own clothes before, and she'd fully expected to do the chore.

The good girl in her prodded her to offer to take over, but the frightened rabbit she'd become in the past few hours ordered her to get away while she could. She slid past him, intent on going to her room and bolting the door.

"Where are you going?" he asked over his shoulder.

She stopped and angled a look at him. Muscles played across his bare back, tapering at a lean waist. The gun stuck out of his belt.

"To bed," she whispered.

He nodded, and relief relaxed the tension in her neck and shoulders. "Don't close the door."

"What?" The word came out a mere squeak.

His eyebrows slanted together in an ominous *V.* "Believe me, I will break it down."

AFTER THROWING another log into the fire, Cord wrung out his shirt, fastened the top two buttons in the hope of retaining some shape and then stretched the shirt out near the stone fireplace so that it would be dry by morning.

His jeans could've used a good washing, too, but not in that small basin. He'd worry about them tomorrow night. If he was still here. In Deadwood. In 1878.

Sweat filmed the back of his neck. He'd never been so baffled in his entire life. What was he supposed to do from here? Was there a purpose to being sucked back into time? Or had the incident been a freak of nature? Or maybe this was some cosmic joke, being sent back to a time where Indians were both feared and hated. Was the key to returning linked to finding the two sisters? Was this his penance for turning his back on the Dine?

If he could only clear his head long enough to think straight. What she'd told him about the woman who'd been labeled a whore didn't necessarily rule out the fact that she could be Reese Winslow. A respected doctor in the future, sure, but how she was regarded here would be a different matter. He didn't even know if women doctors existed during this time.

But he did know that Indians were being farmed to reservations, or had been bribed into scouting for the whites, and with the exception of a few who'd migrated to Washington and wormed their way into politicians' pockets, had no place in polite society. Hard as it was, he had to keep that in mind when he glimpsed the terror in Maggie's eyes. She was a lone woman, for God's sake. How did he expect her to act?

He still wasn't sure if she really had a father, who could come crawling out of the woodwork at any minute. Just when Cord had convinced himself that the guy didn't exist, she'd speak of him so naturally that it made Cord stop and think again. His guess was that the guy was away, prospecting just like she said, but far enough away that he wouldn't be showing up anytime soon. The place was run-down enough that the man obviously wasn't a farmer, so it fit that he could be chasing gold just like most of the male population of Deadwood.

Even inside the small cabin, furniture was sparse. Only one rocking chair sat by the fire, and a colorful braided rug made from a hodgepodge of scrap material laid out in front. A plain cedar chest was pushed up against the wall and topped with a neatly folded quilt. Cord used the open space between the rocker and the kitchen table to stretch out his back and neck, and then did a couple of squats to loosen his thigh muscles. His whole body ached, and not just from the plane ride this morning. Hard to believe he'd been in L.A. less than twenty-four hours ago.

The girls couldn't have vanished into thin air.

Leslie's offhand remark spoken just yesterday taunted him. Made him dig deep for an explanation that seemed too fantastic to accept. Time was linear. A human being had no capacity for screwing with it. Yet people believed in a God they couldn't see or hear or touch. What if this God sometimes changed the rules? In every religion he was familiar with, God was all-powerful, all-seeing. If His plan wasn't being followed, couldn't He change the course of time? Or a person's destiny?

Put things to right as He saw fit?

Hell, it had been so long since Cord considered what he

personally believed, that it was hard to wrap his brain around anything prescribed or mystical. He stared into the flames, remembering long-ago nights around Masi's cook fire while she spoke lovingly of Mother Earth and Sky Father and the importance of living in harmony with nature. That he understood, but why couldn't he grasp her unshaken belief that the spirit didn't die? That every man's journey held purpose?

He rubbed his weary eyes. All that philosophizing was too deep for him right now. Tomorrow would be soon enough to tax his brain. He had to go to town and dig around, find out about this so-called runaway whore. Maggie was so scared she was likely to tell him anything she thought she would get him to leave.

His gaze went to the bedroom door. She'd left it open as he'd instructed, but only by a crack. He'd already eyeballed the room and there was a window in there, only barely large enough for her to crawl through. If she'd tried, he would've heard her. There were also two cots, side by side, about three feet apart.

That was another reason he'd doubted the existence of her phantom father. Where did the man sleep? Surely not in the same room with her. Cord didn't care how cramped the place was or about the attitude of the time, the idea creeped him out. Ironic, since he had every intention of crawling in there with her himself as soon as she'd settled down.

He didn't have much choice, except to sleep on the hard wood floor, and with his shoulder acting up, he'd be in sorry shape come morning. The narrowness of the cot put its appeal only a step above the floor, since it was meant for someone under six feet. Pushed together, they would accommodate both her and his six-foot-three frame.

Obviously Maggie wasn't going to like his plan, but he had a more compelling reason for the sleeping arrangement. If he kept her trapped against the wall, he wouldn't have to worry about her sneaking out, or awake to find himself looking down the barrel of the sheriff's rifle.

He listened more intently, hoping to hear the even sound of her breathing. Fear might have kept her awake for a while, but the same fear tended to create exhaustion. He waited just outside the door a few more minutes, thought he heard the soft sound of slumber, and then pulled off his boots and slid out of his jeans, deciding it wise to keep on his underwear. Although the air was cool, more for her sake than his, he grabbed the quilt off the chest and wrapped it around his waist.

At the doorway, he braced himself for creaking hinges, but a gentle push and the door opened smoothly. Enough light spilled in from the fireplace behind him that he could see her slight form huddled beneath a quilt against the far wall, her back to him. Only the tops of her shoulders were visible. Not surprising, she still wore the blue dress. But she'd released her hair from the bun and the long curly auburn tresses fanned out over the pillow, overflowing the edge of the cot.

At some point she'd awake to find him beside her, and she'd be angry and scared, but if he could grab just a couple of hours of sleep first, maybe she'd acknowledge that was all he wanted, that he meant no harm.

He treaded lightly, stopping twice to make sure he hadn't awoken her. When he got to the spare cot, he hunkered down and lifted the corner off the floor and swung it silently toward hers. He paused, relieved she hadn't stirred, and then grasped the other end. Settling it in place, leaving less than an inch between the two cots, he bunched the quilt around his body. He didn't even make it down before she jackknifed off her cot, and screamed.

MAGGIE CLUTCHED the quilt to her bosom, her lungs aching from the terrified shrieks wracking her body. She'd forgotten it was him. That the Indian was in her house. In her bedroom. Remembering didn't help. His big body was a foot from hers, blocking out the light that should have filtered in from the fireplace.

"Shh, Maggie, I won't hurt you." He put a hand on her shoulder and she thought she would faint.

She jerked wildly away from his touch and screamed louder.

"Maggie!" he shouted. "Stop it." He lunged across both cots, and put a hand over her mouth. "Be quiet and I'll let you go."

She couldn't breathe. Not because of his hand. He wasn't pressing tightly, but panic blocked her airway. She bucked and gasped for air. Immediately he withdrew his hand. But not before she caught his little finger between her teeth and bit down hard.

He let out a vicious curse and abruptly drew back, shaking out his hand. Quickly turning her cheek, she braced herself for his fist, more sobs building in her throat.

The blow never came. She sputtered, still struggling for air, and then hiccupped, and dared a look in his direction.

"Guess I deserved that," he muttered, probing his finger. "I thought warning you would be worse. My mistake."

"Wh-what are you doing in here?" Had she actually slept? How could she possibly have fallen asleep knowing he was in the cabin?

"There are only two cots."

"I know that," she snapped. "You still can't be in here."

"I already am."

"Take the cot. Put it near the fire. That's where Pa sleeps."

"Yeah, but your pa doesn't have to worry about you sneaking out or clobbering him while he's sleeping."

To her horror, Cord straightened the cot so that it butted up to hers again.

"Relax, Maggie." He sighed tiredly as he sat on the edge of the cot, shifting, as if testing how it would take his weight.

"I've never forced a woman to do anything she didn't want to do. All I want is some sleep."

Under the quilt, she drew her knees up to her chest and tried to put as much distance between herself and Cord as possible. The back of her head hit the wall with a thud. She winced. "Where you come from, or according to your culture, it might be okay to be in a woman's room, but here it's not. It's…it's indecent."

Through the hazy light she saw one side of his mouth curve, and his teeth gleam white. "Where I come from, a woman usually invites me into her room." He shrugged a naked shoulder. "A few have even begged."

She gasped in outrage, suddenly noticing that his shirt was not the only thing lacking. She could see his brown bare legs where the quilt he'd draped around him ended. "You're despicable."

"Sometimes, that, too. Right now I'm just tired." He lay back and stretched out, the quilt bunched around his middle. His shoulders were so broad, they spread beyond his cot onto hers.

She cowered closer to the wall, but there was nowhere to go. "Why not take the cot outside, close the door and sleep up against it?"

"You'll crawl through the window."

"I can't. It's too small."

"See? You already tried."

She glared at him, angry with herself when her gaze stubbornly went to the breadth of his bare shoulders.

"I'm too tall for one cot." He shifted, so that his feet no longer dangled off his own cot, but imposed upon hers.

"Merciful heaven," she muttered, incredulousness edging away some of the fear. "You can't be serious about this."

"Shh." He threw the back of his arm across his eyes.

In spite of herself, her gaze wandered over his strong chest, where faint moonlight splashed through the window. Some of his ribs poked out, but mostly the muscle bunched and mounded and thoroughly fascinated her. His skin was dark enough that in the muted light she had to strain to see the brown flat circles around his nipples. Something funny happened to her insides.

"Maggie?"

She flinched and averted her gaze, even though he didn't draw his arm away from his eyes, and held her breath.

"Lie down. Try to sleep."

Her nerves were tauter than Mr. Morrow's fiddle strings, and this man expected her to sleep? She exhaled slowly, curled up as tightly as she could and tucked the quilt around her legs and bottom. But she was too tall, her legs too long to hold the cramped position for long, and she had to stretch out her feet a little.

Her only consolation was that Cord seemed genuinely exhausted, and maybe he did mean to leave her alone. He just didn't trust that she wouldn't flee if given the opportunity. Which is exactly what she would do if he didn't have her cornered. Still, he hadn't hurt her in any way, she reasoned, her heart rate slowing. Maybe it wasn't his fault that he wasn't a decent sort of fellow. He was a heathen, after all. Wearing white man's clothes didn't automatically make him civilized.

But he had perfect diction, no Indian accent at all. His mother was likely white and had taught him well. And if he were a Pinkerton, he had to do a pretty good job to afford the nice clothes he wore. Her gaze went back to his naked chest, and she drew an uneven breath. Truly he needn't have undressed to go to sleep. That she didn't understand one bit. She flexed one cramped calf muscle and then the other.

"Damn it." He sat up, lightning fast, and grabbed both her ankles. She let out a shriek. He pulled her feet out so that she had no choice but to slump back as he dragged her to a lying position. "Now, would you quit fidgeting and go to sleep," he growled, and threw an arm around her waist.

7

MAGGIE COULDN'T BREATHE. She tried frantically to gulp down air. But the burning in her lungs made her feel as if she were drowning, like the time she'd been thrown from her pa's gelding when she was eleven, and ended up in the creek behind the school in Lincoln, outside of Kansas City.

Her fingernails dug into flesh, and she raised her shoulders off the cot, but no matter what she did it seemed as if she were unable to get enough air down her windpipe.

He eased some of the pressure of his arm across her middle, but the truth was, he hadn't been pressing hard enough to cause this reaction. She slapped at his shoulder, her palm tingling where it met his warm flesh.

"Maggie, calm down. You think I'm gonna let you go when you're acting like this?" He'd rolled over to his side, bracing his head up with one hand.

"I can't breathe."

"Yes, you can."

"Don't tell me whether I can breathe or not." As soon as she said the words she knew that air had managed to again soothingly fill her lungs. The rhythm of drawing in and then exhaling wasn't yet normal, but as long as he was this close she didn't expect otherwise.

"You all right?"

"No."

His chuckle stirred her hair and tickled the skin near her ear. When he moved his hand, she thought he would release her, but he only tucked the quilt more snugly under her arm, leaving the weight of his arm across her middle.

She squeezed her eyes shut. "Please."

"Have I hurt you?" he whispered.

She nodded.

"Where?"

Her pride stung like crazy. That counted for more than a bruise. "Do you have to *touch* me?"

He flinched, and then in a dangerously soft voice, whispered, "I'll take my filthy heathen hands off you, but if you run, if you make a single move to leave this cot, don't expect me to be a gentleman."

She swallowed hard, and briefly closed her eyes, as he roughly pulled away and flopped onto his back. She hadn't meant anything unkind about him being an Indian. Being a man was quite enough. But she decided it best to say no more.

Taking his threat seriously, she laid stiffly for several moments, wondering if it would be better to roll onto her side and face the wall, or stay where she was and keep a watchful eye. She decided lying perfectly still was her best move for now. Truth be told, he'd only touched her to keep her in place.

It was hardly an excuse for his rude actions, but she understood what she must do if she truly wanted to be left alone.

The minutes ticked by with excruciating slowness while she waited and listened but was soon rewarded with a subtle change in his breathing. He hadn't lied about needing sleep. Exhaustion had claimed him quickly. Except for the slight parting of his lips, he'd barely moved, she noticed as she ever so slightly cocked her head toward him.

Because he needed the foot of her cot to be able to stretch out, his head and upper body angled away from her. Bending her knees, careful not to disturb his feet, she rolled onto her side and stared at his strong profile. Every feature was bold and proud, from his square jaw, to his long straight nose, to the dimple in his chin. Even his lashes were long and thick, a total waste for a man.

Or maybe not. She swallowed around the sudden obstruction in her throat. Being this close, unabashedly watching him in private like this, made her insides quiver like the leaves of a quaking aspen in a brisk breeze. In fact, her body seemed to be experiencing all kinds of physical things that were foreign to her. Sure, thanks to her fair skin, she flushed more readily than she liked, but the heat never seeped down to her bosom and reached all the way to her belly like it did now.

Oddly, the feeling wasn't entirely unpleasant. Even more odd, the fear had subsided, the knots of tension at the base of her skull slowly uncoiling. Maybe because in sleep he looked so harmless. He even looked handsome.

She gave a small shake of her head, and then froze again when his mouth and chin moved slightly. His eyes stayed closed though, and within seconds, she felt comfortable resuming her visual exploration, amazed at the unexpected urge to peer closer still.

She'd never really studied a man's lips before and she tried hard to recall if it was common for the lower lip to be that much fatter than the top one. As smooth and hairless as his chest was, his face was heavily shadowed with dark stubble that stopped rather sharply at his throat. One day's growth of whiskers had made Pa look old and messy, but on Cord, well, it didn't look bad at all. At the side of his neck, his ebony hair wasn't so straight, not like she expected of an Indian. Lying here like he was, his hair seemed longer than when he was standing, and curled a bit at the ends, toward his jutting collarbone.

The glow of a struggling moon doled out a measly amount

of light and, frustrated, she leaned toward Cord's chest for a better view. His slow even breathing danced across her cheek and made the confines of the layers of muslin she wore unbearably warm. It didn't help that she'd donned an extra petticoat for her trip to town. But she wasn't about to try and remove it now and risk waking him. Besides, the more layers, the more protection.

She nearly laughed out loud at herself. Why she would spend a moment fretting over her virtue she had no idea. It was silly, really, to think he'd be interested in a tall, skinny redhead like her. He hadn't shown a spark of interest, and if he had, she would've thought him dimwitted. She had no exceptional features to recommend her, only freckles, too many to count. She'd stopped trying at thirteen. No, Clara was the beauty of the family, Pa had said, and of course he was right.

Maggie's gaze went to Cord's splayed hand, which was definitely larger than hers, another novelty for her, and she had the sudden urge to press her palm against his and measure to be sure. Not that she would ever behave in such an unladylike manner, but the thought alone brought the feeling of butterflies flittering about inside her belly.

Drawing in a ragged breath, she went back to staring at his mouth, and then the rise and fall of his chest as he breathed. The minutes dragged on and as much as she found that she liked watching him, she knew this wouldn't do. She wasn't going to get a wink of sleep, she thought, and yawned hugely. Although she could at least try. She closed her eyes and yawned again, feeling the tension of the day begin to seep from her pores.

CORD AWOKE SLOWLY, the remnants of a dream lingering at the edge of his consciousness. This time the twilight vision had nothing to do with Masi, or at least not the mental glimpses he strained to remember. It had been about the ocean—vast, endless, its blue-green depths a balm to his restless spirit.

Anything is possible.

He abruptly opened his eyes, certain he'd heard the words spoken aloud. The unfamiliar ceiling was rough and unfinished. Pinkish-gray light cloaked his face, a breeze coming in through an open window felt crisp and cool on his chin and neck. A mass of auburn curls fell across his shoulder. A palm rested idly on his belly, while a long slender leg had been casually thrown over his.

Memory crept through his mind with the stealth of a prowling cougar. Keeping his head still, he slid a gaze toward his sleeping companion.

Maggie.

She looked remarkably young when her face wasn't pinched with fear. Early twenties was his guess. Her skin was fair, almost translucent, yet she had no premature age lines from the harsh sun and wind. Her bow-shaped lips were still plump with youth, and so far creases had spared her cheeks of grooves, or the skin at the corners of her eyes from crow's-feet.

Tempted to brush back the curl that corkscrewed over one closed eye, he did his best to stay still. She looked so peaceful, sound asleep as she was. But as soon as she realized that under the quilt her one hand had sought warmth beneath his thigh, or that her other hand rested an inch above his thickening cock, she'd be jumping around like a cat who'd just had his tail stampeded by a herd of cattle.

He closed his eyes again and smiled, even though he'd tried not to. When he was certain he hadn't disturbed her, he opened his eyes again and moved his head a fraction of an inch, just enough so that he could see how long her hair extended. The long loose auburn curls were everywhere. Unbound, the tresses had to reach her waist.

She moved her hand, the one closest to his cock, and he shut his eyes again, trying not to react. But he'd instinctively sucked in his belly, bracing himself for an accidental brush of her fingers or, worse, the groping unconsciousness of sleep.

She made a small whimpering sound, and snuggled closer, which did nothing to fortify his self-control. Every muscle in his body tensed, his nerves suddenly so taut he didn't know how much longer he could lie motionless. If she had the slightest idea what she'd done, she'd die a thousand deaths in the space of a single heartbeat.

He inhaled shallowly, though still managed to draw in the scent of her…musky, feminine, too heady for his own good. Other than her cheek and the side of her neck, he couldn't see much more of her. Just as well because the sight of her pale skin stirred an oddly primal feeling in his chest, made his belly knot with longing. Maybe because he didn't see skin that milky-white anymore. Certainly not in L.A., where women tended to go from poolside to tanning beds, loath to so much as allow a single tan line to show.

Why did she still have that damn dress on from yesterday? He suddenly wanted to feel her soft white skin against his bare flesh. Naturally he understood why she'd kept herself trussed up like that, but that did nothing to lessen his frustration.

At his sides, his hands reflexively curled into fists, his eyes still closed as he mentally recited an old Indian war chant he'd learned when he'd first moved to the reservation and had thought being Navajo was a cool thing. He wasn't even sure he remembered the English translation for the entire chant but it didn't matter. The mindless repetition was doing its job, slowly putting him in that meditative state that allowed him to shut her out.

Yet a few minutes later, he knew the exact instant she awoke. She didn't react right away. Awareness of him, where she was, where her hands rested, obviously took longer to sink in. Cord remained motionless, faking sleep, so that she could reposition herself, hopefully maintain some measure of dignity. Even when she gasped, and jerked her hand away from his belly, he didn't so much as let an eyelash flicker.

After that, it was the blind waiting, the tense silence that nearly drove him over the edge. She hadn't bolted upright, or flew off the cot as he'd prepared himself for. Or even screamed. Instead, she stayed immobile herself, leaving her hand wedged beneath his thigh. Maybe she was afraid more movement would wake him.

That theory was quickly shot to hell when he felt her shift, her soft round breast suddenly pressing against his bicep. He nearly opened his eyes then, but refrained when he felt her warm moist breath touch his jaw. The idea that she'd actually snuggled closer almost made him smile.

Well, well, what happened to all that crap about the impropriety of a lady being alone with a man? And an Indian, no less. Annoyance over her two-faced sensibilities made it hard for him to keep his cool, but smug satisfaction won out. He wouldn't move until he saw where she was headed with her game.

Something hovered near his face and his curiosity abruptly turned to alarm. Was she about to clobber him while he was daydreaming? He opened his eyes, tense and ready. Her eyes widened with shock, her hand suspended above his chin, the tip of her finger lightly touching his lower lip.

Her sharp intake of breath broke the silence. Before she could snatch her hand back, he smiled and drew her finger into his mouth.

HORRIFIED, MAGGIE only stared, her entire body frozen still, her finger in his mouth all the way to the knuckle. He suckled it like a babe would suckle its mother's breast. As for her, she couldn't think. Her insides felt like mush, her legs too rubbery to hold her up if she tried to stand.

She yanked back her hand and tried to crawl to the foot of her cot. He caught her arm, and as if she weighed no more than a rag doll, jerked her toward him. She flailed her free arm, trying to find the windowsill, this time working up a good shriek, but another tug and she flew toward him, her palm flattening on his hard muscular chest.

His arm clamped around her waist, and with his other hand, he cradled the back of her head, urging her face to his raised one until their lips met, cutting her off in midscream. Stunned, it eventually occurred to her that she should still be struggling. She shoved wildly against him, pressing the heel of her hand against his hardened nipple.

He smiled against her mouth, and then withdrew a scant inch. "I thought you wanted to play."

The strangled cry that escaped her tight lips sounded more animal than human.

His lips slackened against hers, and then he trailed them to her jaw. "Will you be quiet?"

She screamed again.

His mouth came back to hers, more forcefully this time, the hand at the back of her head keeping her right where he wanted her. His lips started out firm, but softened and then parted coaxingly. The tip of his tongue touched the seam of hers, and she could feel his heart beat against her breastbone.

Panic rose in her throat. He wasn't hurting her. In fact, the feel of his warm muscled body actually felt oddly pleasant.

And yet, this was so foreign, so... "Stop," she whispered against his mouth. "Please."

Abruptly, he pulled back. "No screaming, and stay where you are."

Sprawled across his body? Right. She took a fortifying breath and then lunged over him, and landed on the floor beside his cot, her right knee hitting the hard planks with a painful thud. Before she could get up, he was standing beside her, his long fingers wrapped around her upper arms as he hauled her to her feet.

He sighed and shoved his other hand through his thick dark hair. The quilt that had covered his body still lay half on the cot, half on the floor. The only thing he wore were drawers. Odd, short fancy drawers that looked like silk, that showed off thighs and calves every bit as powerfully built as his chest and arms. "This is way too early for this."

She tried to back away from him but he wouldn't give an inch. "What are you going to do with me?"

His eyebrows went up. "What were you about to do to me?"

"Nothing," she said quickly, feeling the guilty flush climb her neck. She looked away and, thankfully, he allowed her the reprieve. "I promise I— Nothing," she repeated in a small voice. What *had* she been thinking? Touching him like that? She couldn't very well admit to her curiosity. "I have to go outside for a moment," she muttered finally, hoping he wouldn't make her announce her need to visit the outhouse.

When he didn't respond, she looked up and found him staring at the tangled cascade of red hair that fell over her shoulder and down her breast, and nearly touched her waist. She took a self-conscious swipe at it, realizing what an awful fright the unruly mop of curls must have given him.

"Don't." He stopped her from pushing the heavy swath back over her shoulder. "It's pretty."

That startled a laugh out of her, and for that instant she forgot he was her enemy. "It's red."

He took a thick strand and rubbed it between his thumb and forefinger. "Soft." A smile tugged at the corners of his mouth. "And it's auburn, not red. Big difference."

The funny fluttering thing happened in her chest again as she watched him play with her hair, letting it coil around his forefinger, fascinated with the way the curl seemed to learn the shape of him. Auburn, he'd called the color, not red. She started to smile and then his meaning dawned like a blustery winter morning.

God help her— His sudden interest in her hair—did he mean to scalp her?

She snatched the strand from him and drew all of her hair back, fisting it in her hand protectively behind her head. "I really have to go outside," she said tightly.

His brows drew together in a slight frown, his eyes boring into hers for a dreadfully long moment. His features slowly tightened, and something that looked like hurt flared and died just as quickly. "Let's go."

She was so taken aback by his reaction, she didn't even object when he held her arm and guided her toward the front door. She barely registered the fact that he was almost naked walking alongside her. Did he know what she'd been thinking? She gave the matter further consideration and decided she was being silly. For goodness' sakes, he wasn't *that* kind of Indian. No doubt she had more to fear from those randy miners who came to town twice a week.

She stopped where her boots lay on the floor. Should she say something? Clear the air? Or was that silly, too?

"No shoes," he said. "I don't want you running."

She didn't like the idea of going out there barefooted. "I just—" She cleared her throat. "I'm not used to compliments." Without waiting for a response, she quickly turned toward the door. She wouldn't fight him on the shoes. She wouldn't win, anyway.

He hesitated, and then grabbed the trousers he'd left draped over a kitchen chair and stepped into them. Leaving the denim unsnapped, he picked up the gun and opened the door. They walked side by side in silence, her picking around the rocks that lay on the dusty ground. Walking with bare feet didn't seem to bother him any but he stayed abreast of her until they got to the privy.

"I'll be right out here," he said.

She nodded and went inside to do her business. When she came out, she knew he would be done, too, and it suddenly didn't matter that she wouldn't have the tiny opportunity to escape. He'd had plenty of time to take any kind of liberty he wanted, but he hadn't, even when she'd been foolish enough to invite trouble by her uncensored feminine curiosity.

The knowledge lifted fear off her weighted shoulders, and when she walked back out into the early morning sunlight, her thoughts blessedly went to the mundane chores she still had to do, such as milking Matilda, watering the horses and scattering feed for the chickens.

And then she saw him, standing several yards away, a good half a foot taller than herself, shirtless, his trousers still unsnapped, all smooth light brown skin and lean powerful muscle.

Heaven help her, but her knees felt suspiciously weak, and she thought she just might faint.

8

CORD NARROWED his gaze on Maggie. Was it his imagination, or had she just swayed? "Are you okay?"

She pressed the back of her hand to her forehead. "I think so," she said, and started to crumple.

He lurched toward her and caught her in his arms before she hit the ground. She vaguely waved him away, but he easily picked her up without a struggle and held her against his chest as he carried her back to the cabin.

Although she was tall, she was slim with small fragile bones and he didn't have to strain his injured shoulder to get her back inside. He headed straight for the bedroom because he figured it was easier to set her down on one of the cots, but she made a small whimpering sound and started to wiggle as they passed the kitchen.

"I got a little light-headed but I'm fine now," she said, gesturing for him to set her down. "I have to get the fire started and make coffee."

"I can handle the fire." Reluctantly, he lowered her feet to the floor. "You should loosen those buttons."

Her hand flew defensively to the row of tiny buttons that fastened her dress close to her throat as she stared wide-eyed at him.

"You probably could use the breathing room." He'd never been self-conscious about his body, naked or otherwise, but standing in unsnapped jeans and without a shirt under her curious assessment made him vaguely uncomfortable. He cleared his throat. "That snug collar might've been the problem."

She moistened her lips, her gaze going to her curled toes. "And you shouldn't have picked me up like that," she said, mirroring his discomfort. "You could have hurt yourself."

"What? A tiny thing like you?"

She couldn't quite hide her smile and blushed as she turned to the kettle and the small canister where she kept the coffee. Her hair hung down her back, some of it in big loopy curls that skimmed the top of her waist, the shorter strands on the sides more tightly wound. He hoped she didn't put it back up in that annoying bun. Maybe she wouldn't once she convinced herself he wasn't going to scalp her....

Just thinking of the accusing look on her face earlier made his stomach churn. Man, he had to quit being so touchy. The threat of Indian attacks was real during this time period. These people had just gotten over Custer and his men being wiped out, and whether they deserved it or not wasn't the point.

He checked his shirt, which was dry as a bone, and briefly wondered about a dunk in the river. He had to clean up somehow, and he knew she didn't have a bath house.

"I'll make some breakfast after I get the water on for coffee," she said over her shoulder, her eyes going to his shirt. "You can wash up while I make a pan of biscuits and—" She quickly tied an apron around her waist, her voice dropping shyly. "And then I'll take a turn at the washbasin. Maybe later you can help me bring in the washtub from the barn."

"I plan on leaving by early afternoon."

"Oh. To town. Right." She nodded and hurried past him into the bedroom.

He frowned, not sure if he should follow her. Check on

what she suddenly seemed hell-bent on doing. "But I'll help you carry the tub in here before I go."

She reappeared, her hair coiled at her nape, while poking pins into the messy bun she'd formed. "I can do that myself, thank you. I'm used to it."

So why didn't her father help her? Cord decided not to ask. Better to leave it alone and give her that small measure of security. Yet if there were a man in the picture... His gaze went back to the blue-and-white striped Egyptian cotton shirt. Talk about sticking out like a sore thumb. "Look, I don't suppose your father would have an old shirt I could borrow for the day."

Her lips parted in surprise, her gaze lingered on his bare shoulders. "You'd never fit in his things. He's an inch shorter than me, and you're a good deal broader and more—" She cut herself off, her embarrassed gaze briefly lifting to his face before she rushed past him. "Although Pa was getting a bit of a paunch and the shirt I started making him for Christmas, well, I left it a little roomy the way he liked it." She kept her face averted and went to the chest sitting against the wall.

Curious, he moved to stand behind her as she unfastened the latch and opened the chest. To his amazement, there actually was a neatly folded pile of men's clothes, as well as some knickknacks, some needlepoint and what looked like skirts and a fancy bonnet.

"Going on a trip?" he asked.

She pulled out something brown and flannel, and quickly slammed the chest closed. "I believe I may have mentioned that I'm going to visit my sister in San Francisco. In fact, she and her husband should be here any day to fetch me." She shrugged a shoulder and swept past him with the shirt in her hand. "It could even be this afternoon."

Cord smiled to himself. The packed chest was proof enough of her claim, but that she still tried so hard to make him believe she wasn't out here alone made him wonder. "So you think that might fit me?"

She went to the table where she kept her sewing, her gaze trained on the flannel. "I'll have to do something about adding to the sleeves."

"Maybe I should try it on first?"

"Oh, yes, of course." She gave a curt nod and held the garment out at arm's length without looking at him.

He took the scratchy shirt from her and held it up against his body, already knowing it was going to be too short, also knowing that tucking it in would help. At his height, he often had trouble with off-the-rack clothes, but he'd learned early on, when he'd been a tall gangly teenager with no money for custom fits, how to adapt.

Upon closer inspection he realized there were no button holes yet, or buttons, and that one of the sleeves was pinned on but not yet sewn. He slid an arm into the finished sleeve, and then more carefully into the other. The shoulder area was too snug, and when he gave too firm a tug to adjust the fabric, a sharp pin dragged across his skin. Just in time, he bit back a curse.

"Oh, dear." Maggie put out a hand. "I forgot about the pins."

"My fault. I saw them." He gingerly tried to disengage himself from the sharp points.

"Let's see." She plucked the fabric away from him, drawing her lower lip under her teeth. "If you could just hold still, I could see where I need to alter the shirt."

"Go ahead. I'm tough."

She smiled shyly, suddenly looking as if she didn't know what to do with her hands. Her tongue darted out and swept the area she'd nibbled. Finally, she squared her shoulders, shoved back the errant curls that clung to her cheek and, with her gaze pinned to the right sleeve, used her finger to measure the distance from where the cuff ended to his wrist.

He didn't know how she managed to do it without actually touching him, but she obviously took great pain to avoid contact. She was like a totally different woman from the one who'd snuggled up to him this morning. He didn't get it.

"I can fix this," she said, her voice throaty, her eyelids deliberately lowered. "It'll be a little patchy but I can make sure to blend the plaid pattern so that it doesn't show too much."

"I'm sure you'll do a great job. Thank you."

Her green eyes were bright and probing in her heart-shaped face. Without the aid of cosmetics, even her thick lashes were a dark auburn. Her nose was pert and upturned, the freckles sprinkled liberally, and her lips were a natural pink that lifted at the corners. She was a lot prettier than at first glimpse. Mostly though, it was the emerald color and almond shape of her eyes that made her stand out.

She let out a shaky breath. Fear had crept back into her eyes, turning them a darker shade. Maggie had probably never been this close to a man before. A woman her age should be married. With kids. Lots of them. Unless she was widowed, which would account for her living with her father. Could this morning have been about simple curiosity?

"Maggie." He lightly touched her arm.

She jumped. "I'm a fairly good seamstress." Her face flooded with pink. "Not to boast, mind you. That's what Pa says. I reckon the added material won't be too noticeable."

They both heard it at the same time. The fall of hooves pounding dirt.

Maggie spun around. Cord's gaze flew to the open window. Enough dust had kicked up so that he couldn't see how many riders approached. His guess was only one horse made the noise, a horse being ridden fairly fast. Not a good sign.

Frowning, she moved to the window, and looked out before glancing at him over her shoulder. Their eyes met for a long painful exchange. This was her chance to get rid of Cord. No reason she shouldn't grab it. "It's the deputy," she announced. "Go to the bedroom and close the door. I'll try to keep him outside."

At first, Cord thought he'd misheard. "Maggie, I want you to know I've done nothing wrong but I don't—"

"Go," she ordered, heading for the door, stopping to smooth back her hair before grasping the doorknob. At the last moment, she grabbed the unloaded rifle before opening the door.

Confused and uncertain, he lingered, seriously considering listening near the window, but then he ran the risk of the deputy stepping inside the cabin and asking questions Cord couldn't answer. He had no choice but to trust her and do as she instructed. But he took his own shirt with him into the room. If he ended up in jail, at least he'd be comfortable.

"GOOD MORNING, Deputy, what brings you out this way in such a hurry?" Maggie had never liked Lester. He had mean, shifty eyes and an insolent smile that set her teeth on edge on the few occasions she'd found herself alone with him.

Lester dismounted, his beady gaze darting to the carbine she held in her hands. "Mornin', Miz Dawson. Your pa inside?"

"No, I'm afraid you just missed him."

He tethered his horse to the porch post, which really riled her. Having just been told her pa was gone, he had no business expecting to stay. "Gone prospecting?"

"Yes."

"I heard he was still ailing."

"He started feeling better last night."

Lester turned briefly to spit onto the dusty ground. Another of his habits that she detested. "Got a mighty early start, I see."

She nodded. "He's been under the weather for a while so

he got restless. Is there a message I can give him?" she asked as pleasantly as she was able.

He smiled that horrible oily smile of his. "Mostly I wanted to check on you, make sure you were all right, Miz Dawson."

She deliberately ran her palm down the barrel of the Spencer carbine. "You shouldn't have troubled yourself, Deputy. Even when Pa is away for a day or two, I do fine when I'm on my own. Pa's been teaching me how to shoot."

"Has he now?" Lester's gaze went to the rifle before flickering to the front of her dress and lingering on her breasts, and making her shift uncomfortably.

"Yes, and he said my aim is good and steady, and for the last two weeks I haven't missed my practice target once." All these lies were going to send Maggie straight to hell. Yet surely God wouldn't want her vulnerable to the likes of Lester.

She wasn't the only one in town who didn't like the man. He had a reputation for being a coward and a back-shooter, and some folks were convinced he'd been hiding in the Golden Slipper the day the sheriff had been gunned down in front of the jailhouse. Fine thing since they'd been boyhood friends, which was the only reason Lester had gotten the job as deputy in the first place. Rumor had it that the new sheriff was fixing to get rid of Lester.

He took off his hat, slapped it against his thigh, sending up a cloud of dust, and propped a booted foot on the first step.

Lord have mercy, he couldn't mean to stay any longer. She took a hasty step toward him, hoping he'd catch on that he wasn't welcome inside. If she had to, she'd walk right past him to the barn to draw him away from the cabin. But the mere thought of getting any closer to him than she absolutely had to made her skin crawl as if she'd been plagued by a swarm of locusts.

He reared his head back at her rudeness. "If it's not too much trouble, Miz Dawson, I sure wouldn't mind a cup of your fine strong coffee."

"Normally, Deputy, I'd be happy to oblige, but Pa finished the last of it before he left, and I have my chores to do."

Lester turned and spit again. This time when he looked at her, that hint of meanness that often lurked in his long narrow face cast a warning shadow that made the back of her neck clammy. "Where's your Pa prospecting these days?"

She forced a small laugh. "He doesn't discuss such things with me."

"Nah, reckon he wouldn't."

Relief spilled through her. The last thing she wanted to do was get into a discussion about where Pa's gold came from. Lord only knew she'd told enough lies, but that was a secret she'd take to her grave. She'd promised Pa Mary would be the only one to whom Maggie would confide.

"If you'll excuse me, Deputy. I really do need to get to the barn." She took another cautious step down from the porch.

Finally he slid his boot to the dirt and straightened to his normal bow-legged stance. "You best keep that rifle with you whenever you come outside."

She blinked warily at him, her pulse picking up speed, as she considered whether that was meant as a threat. "Why?"

"On account of the stagecoach being attacked outside of town yesterday."

"Yesterday?" She gripped the rifle tighter, and nearly spun back toward the cabin to see if Cord was at the window. "When?"

"Early afternoon. About the same time the stage always comes through. Why? You hear something?"

"No, of course not." She smiled, trying to seem nonchalant, even though her thoughts stampeded in three directions. "I was just in town yesterday myself. Didn't hear a thing while I was there or on my way home."

"Reckon you wouldn't have heard nothin'. Happened

about a mile north of town. Damn bold to get that close to Deadwood and attack, you ask me."

"They get anything?"

Lester shook his head. "The driver only seen one fella coming up on the coach from behind. But he only got off two shots before one of the passengers got out a shotgun and returned fire."

"They didn't hit him, though." Maggie felt the blood drain from her face. A lone gunman? No, it didn't mean anything. Cord would've had to have gone through town to meet up with her as quickly as he had, and they would've caught him then.

"Nope, but the passenger, a shopkeeper from Texas, he suspected he mighta nicked the bandit's horse."

She clutched the porch post for support. Why hadn't she wondered why Cord was traveling without a horse?

"You all right, Miz Dawson?"

"Fine." She pressed a hand to her nervous belly. Cord? A would-be stage robber? No, he'd claimed he was a Pinkerton. He was searching for those women. He even had pictures of them.

"You don't look none too fine. Maybe you ought to sit a spell."

She shook her head. "Really, I'm all right." No, she wasn't. Not one bit all right. Bile rose in her throat. She shouldn't jump to conclusions. The clothes Cord wore were too fine for a common robber.

"Miz Dawson," Lester began, his gaze narrowing suspiciously on the cabin door, his hand hovering tensely over his holstered gun. "Might be best I have a look around."

"What?" She snapped back to reality, and waved a hand. She didn't believe that Cord was a criminal. She didn't. He'd given her no reason when he'd had plenty of opportunity. "That's not necessary."

He seemed relieved, the coward. "It's not right your pa leaving you alone so much. Reckon I just might have myself a man-to-man talk with him." Lester put a familiar hand at the small of her back, moving in so close she could see the beginning of yellow tobacco stains on his front teeth.

Her stomach truly revolted then, and she jerked away. Instinctively she knew Cord had nothing to do with the stagecoach attack. She felt nothing like this when he'd touched her. She felt different. Heaven help her, but she'd felt more alive than she ever had before.

"Miz Dawson? Something is powerfully wrong here." His beady eyes darted to the cabin window.

"My pa's been sick, Deputy. I've been the one taking care of him. It would seem I might have a touch of—" She abruptly covered her mouth with her hand, just in time to hide her smile, when she saw the despicable man stumble backward, as far away from her as he could get without running into his horse.

"Maybe I should ask Mrs. Weaver to call on you. Bring by some of her soup."

"Oh, no," Maggie said quickly. "If I am contagious, it's better I don't infect anyone. Anyway, I'm feeling a bit better already. Probably just needed some air."

"It's cool out here. You should go back inside," he said, taking in her blue dress, and then—to her horror—noticing at the same time she did, that her bare toes peeked out from beneath her hem.

She gasped, and then covered it up with a small laugh, while arranging her dress so that her feet didn't show. "You caught me by surprise, Deputy. I'd just been getting dressed to go out to the barn."

Lester eyed her as if she were a feebleminded old biddy. "You need to live in town like a proper lady, Miz Dawson, and not out here by your lonesome so much. You tell your pa that my offer still stands, might even be willing to go up a few dollars." His interest swiftly switched from her to the cabin, his keen gaze sliding briefly toward the creek winding away from the property to the left. "The place ain't much, but I'd be willing to do a little fixin' up."

Ah, so that's what this was about. He still wanted the homestead. She should have known right off. The knowledge gave her no comfort. In fact, it made her shiver. Yet he couldn't know the truth about the gold. If he did, if anyone knew, she'd never be safe here.

"That's something best discussed with Pa," she said curtly, and, holding on to the post, moved back up a step. "Thanks for stopping by, Deputy. I think I will go inside now."

"You take care of yourself, Miz Dawson." He set his hat back on his head but didn't make a move for his tethered horse until she got to the front door. "And tell your pa what I said."

"I'll be sure to do that." She fumbled with the doorknob, loath to release the rifle even for one second, and then finally opened the door, slipped inside and slid the bolt in place. Leaning heavily with her back against the door, she closed her eyes. Moments later, she heard the sound of galloping hooves.

"Thanks."

The quietly spoken word made her heart leap, and her eyes flew open. She'd been so anxious to get rid of Lester that she'd momentarily forgotten about Cord. Her gaze went to the small gun he held in his hand. As much as she despised the deputy, she prayed she hadn't just made the biggest mistake of her life.

9

CORD SAW THE tremor in Maggie's hands, the quivering chin that she bravely tried to hide. He still couldn't believe that she'd covered for him. Especially after the news about the stage that the deputy had brought her. But was she having second thoughts? Is that why she cowered near the door?

He followed her gaze to the .38 he held. Damn, he'd forgotten he'd had it in his hand. He quickly shoved the gun into his waistband behind his back.

"Maggie, I had nothing to do with that stage being attacked. I hope you know that."

She looked so much like she wanted to believe him that raw emotion painfully tightened in his chest. "You were listening."

"I heard some of the conversation. I was going stir-crazy hiding in the room." He smiled. She didn't smile back. "If I were you, I wouldn't believe me. Why should you? I'm a stranger. I held you here against your will." His voice faltered. Yes, he'd actually done that, held this poor woman captive. "I was a jerk. I'm sorry." He scrubbed at his gritty eyes. "I'm leaving. Right now. Just promise me you'll start keeping that rifle loaded."

"No." She shoved off the door, shaking her head.

He caught and held her gaze. "Look, even if you don't know how to use a weapon, with your father away, you can't be here alone without some kind of protection. Just pull the trigger if you need to, and you might get lucky." The thought of her out here alone and defenseless, preyed upon by a robber, or worse, flamed a fierce protectiveness in him he didn't know he possessed. "I'll get you loaded before I leave. Just promise me you'll pull that trigger if the time comes."

This time she did smile slightly. "I know how to use a rifle. I meant that you can't go into town. You're a stranger, with no horse of your own. You know what everyone will assume."

"Not to mention me being an Indian."

She blinked sheepishly. "True."

He couldn't summon annoyance at the frank admission. "What about you, Maggie, why haven't you made the obvious assumption about me?" he asked, curious suddenly. "Like you said, I don't even have a horse."

She looked at him for a minute and then gave him a wide berth on her way to the kitchen. "Truth be told, I don't rightly know."

"You must be wondering about my mode of transportation."

She wrinkled her nose at him.

"It's true. I don't have a horse." What the hell was he doing? How much did he want to tell her, or could he tell to her? A tale so far-fetched he couldn't quite believe it himself.

"Reckon the thought crossed my mind." Her glance flickered in his direction before she brought out two chipped yellow china cups and set them down on the table.

"I haven't ridden a horse in about a year," he said truthfully. "I had an accident and hurt my shoulder, and as you pointed out, I tend to favor my left arm."

"I saw the scar."

"It happened about a year ago," he told her, not keen on discussing the two surgeries that had ended his career. Not that she would understand any of it.

She seemed puzzled and pleased at the same time. "You had a mighty fine doctor tending you if that scar is only a year old."

"I was lucky," he said, and then changed the subject. "I'll admit, I didn't believe you lived here with your father until I heard the deputy mention him."

Pain sliced across her face. She quickly reached for a clean rag and used it to pick the kettle up from the fire. "I don't like that man. I wouldn't trust him as far as I could throw him, even if he does wear a tin star. He only got the deputy's job because he and the last sheriff had been friends since they were knee-high to a grasshopper."

"Still, the man did come out and check on you."

"Check on me?" She sniffed. "He wanted to talk to Pa about—" She briefly eyed Cord. "Well, it doesn't matter. You take milk and sugar in your coffee?"

Amazing. She still trusted him. He smiled. "Nope. Black."

"Good, since I haven't done my milking yet." She poured the dark brew into each of their cups and then spooned a liberal amount of sugar into hers. She wasted no time in returning the kettle to the fire and then took her first sip. "I don't know how a body can function without their morning coffee."

Privately agreeing, he sipped the dark brew. Man, Maggie liked her coffee strong. No wonder she used these small cups. Three shots were enough caffeine for the whole day. Maybe he should've used some sugar.

"Is anything wrong?" she asked.

He shook his head. "Fine."

"I know the cups are old and chipped, but they belonged to my mother and I can't seem to part with them." Looking wistful, she pulled out a kitchen chair but didn't sit down.

"How long ago did you lose her?"

"I was seven."

"Me, too. My mother died when I was seven." The words were out of his mouth before he knew it. He never talked about his parents. Or his grandmother for that matter.

"Do you have brothers and sisters?"

"No, it's just me."

"Your dad's gone, too?" she asked softly, sympathy thickening her voice.

"Yeah. I don't know. He could be dead by now." Cord cleared his throat. He never thought about the old man, and he wasn't going to start now. "Don't do any sewing on your dad's shirt. My own will have to be good enough. I shouldn't wait around that long, anyway."

Her eyes went wide with concern. "You're not still going to town."

"I don't see that I have much choice. Someone may have information about the women I'm looking for."

She worried her lower lip. "Surely you understand, Mr. Braddock, that you'll immediately become a suspect over that stagecoach."

"Can you call me Cord?" He grinned. "After all, we've already slept together."

Her face turned a brilliant shade of red and she abruptly presented her back as she produced an iron skillet, and slammed it down on the surface where she worked. "I'll put on a slab of bacon for breakfast, while I milk Matilda. I can't have you going off without being fed. After that, do as you please."

His grin widened at her flash of redhead temper. "I'm just teasing you, Maggie. Don't be mad."

"You're gonna get your fool head shot off, so I wouldn't be in such high spirits if I were you."

He sobered. "I know." Easier to joke than to think about what he faced ahead. "Here, I have something for you."

She stared at him, her expression clouded with worry he didn't want to analyze. Even after he dug into his pocket and held out some cash, she didn't lower her frightened gaze from his face. "Those men in town, they can be vicious," she said softly. "Maybe I can ask around about those women you're looking for."

Her fear had nothing to do with feeling threatened by him, but rather she feared for him, and that touched him in a way nothing had in a very long time. He wasn't sure the feeling was welcome. "They'll want to know why you're asking." He shook his head. "You don't want anyone knowing I've been here. Take this."

She looked as if she was about to protest, and then glanced down at his outstretched hand and frowned. "What is that?"

Hell. What was wrong with him? He'd forgotten that modern currency would mean nothing here. He fished out the silver half-dollar he always kept in his pocket for luck and the dimes he knew were made from silver. "You can have these melted down. They should be worth something."

She picked up the coins and studied them with a puzzled look on her face. "These look like coins but—" She squinted at them. "Is that a—" Her brows drew sharply together. "That can't be a date."

"Of course not." He smiled humorlessly and dropped the half-dollar and the rest of the dimes in her palm. "I wish I had more you could use, but I'm afraid that's it."

"Use for what." She shoved the coins back into his palm.

"Come on. Take it, Maggie." She stubbornly shook her head. "I've drank your coffee and eaten your food and I'm afraid I'll have to ask to borrow your wagon." He flexed his shoulder. He hadn't had occasion to ride, but he could do so comfortably at this point. "Or maybe your father's horse. Better yet, if you could take me in the wagon and let me off close enough to town I could walk the rest of the way. No one has to know I was ever here."

She seemed almost disappointed, and then she lifted her chin indignantly. "I don't want to be paid. I want to help." She shifted her gaze back to the skillet. "It's my Christian duty, after all."

"You've already done more than I could expect. Especially after the way I treated you last night."

She got out a slab of meat that looked nothing like the nicely packaged, presliced bacon he was used to. "I understand why you felt the need to keep me…confined," she said delicately. "Truth be told, I probably would've run to the sheriff, which would have made everything worse for you."

He watched her prepare the bacon, studying the way she deliberately kept her lashes down, her gaze averted. She wasn't playing at being coy. Maggie was the real deal, and damned if he didn't like that she blushed more than any woman he'd ever known.

He grabbed the cloth she'd used to handle the hot kettle and refilled both their cups. "What changed your mind about me?"

She warily slid him a glance, stiffening when he brushed her arm as he returned the kettle to the fire. "Changed my mind?"

"You could have turned me in to the deputy, but you didn't. Last night you would have been screaming your head off as soon as you heard him approach." He gave her a lazy smile meant to put her at ease, but instead she seemed to fumble alarmingly with the knife before hacking off a slab of pork and laying it in the skillet. "Not that I'd have blamed you."

She briefly touched the top button of her modest collar, which he still thought looked too tight and confining for her long slender neck. But he knew better than to bring it up again. "You could have taken—" She hesitated, moistening her lips and swallowing. "You could have been ungentlemanly but you weren't, and that has to count for something in your character."

The thought of taking advantage of a woman was so foreign to him he reared his head in disgust. "I'm no angel.

I've done things I'm not proud of in my life. But I never would have forced you to—" In his vehement denial, he'd nearly been crude. Lamely, he finished with, "Never."

A haunted look entered her eyes and the deep breath she took made her small high breasts jut. Her attention drew to the slab of sizzling meat and she picked up a fork, but then quickly set it back down. "Heavens, I nearly forgot my chores. I won't be gone long. Though long enough that you can wash up if you like," she said, tossing a look at the water pitcher, the basin—anywhere but his face—and wiping her hands on a towel. "And I'd thank you to check the bacon."

"Maggie, is something wrong?"

"No, nothing at all." She still wouldn't look at him, but hurried toward the door, grabbing her boots along the way and looking as if he'd slapped her.

MAGGIE WOULD HAVE taken her time milking Matilda, but the poor old thing's udders were full and the cow was cranky about having waited so long already. The horses needed no more hay forked down from the loft, which today was a mixed blessing, so after watering them, Maggie glanced at the front door. If Cord had poked his head out to check on her, she hadn't seen him. Hopefully he'd taken her suggestion and used the privacy to get washed up, something she sorely needed to do herself.

Using the back of her wrist to push the clinging hair off her clammy forehead, she picked up her skirt with her other hand and headed toward the bend in the creek. The morning air was cool and still heavy with dew and she normally wore a coat since fall had descended. Even the wool shawl that she kept near the front door would have helped ward off the chill, but she dared not go back inside yet. She wasn't quite ready to face him, lest she find mockery, or far worse, pity in his hazel eyes.

Not that she'd glimpsed anything of the sort earlier, but once her silly words sunk in, no telling how he'd react. Plain, too-tall Maggie with her red hair and freckles tempting any man, much less one as handsome and powerfully built as Cord, was surely laughable. She should be glad of her circumstances, and she was. She was grateful that she invited no unwanted attention. Truly she was. With all her heart.

Preoccupied with her own foolishness, she nearly missed the spot. She stopped at the patch of dirt under a young ponderosa pine, a few yards from her dormant summer garden. After a quick glance over her shoulder, she sank to her knees, relieved that nothing marked the hasty grave but a border of wilted prairie grass that she'd left undisturbed. It had to stay that way, at least for now.

Once Mary arrived, together they could erect a wooden cross to properly mark Pa's passing. Mary would surely want to say a few words as well. But for now, the secret of his death had to be protected. No matter how disrespectful it seemed to allow the span of a man's life to go unremarked.

"Oh, Pa, I'm so sorry. You deserve better," Maggie whispered, her voice catching on a sob as she plowed her fingers through the dirt.

Fresh guilt overcame her when she realized that she had to do something about leaving the newly churned earth in so obvious a bald patch. The fall chill had helped by robbing life from the surrounding grass, causing the brown blades to wilt, but evidence of her own hapless digging was still too noticeable. If Lester had poked around back here, he might have become suspicious. But for her to further disturb her father's resting place…

"This is what you'd want me to do, Pa. I know you would," she said brokenly. "You're not here to take care of me. I have to think for myself. I have to be strong. I have to—"

Without thinking further, she blindly wound the tall dry grass around her scraped knuckles and jerked the blades from the cold ground. Unnourished, the roots came easy. In a matter of a week or two, the frozen dirt would not allow the breach, but for now, it took only a minute to disrupt the pattern of the grave.

She sank back on her heels, her hands filthy, her dress caked with damp dirt. "I'll make this up to you, Pa. I promise I will. As soon as Mary comes. Maybe we'll even get a marker from town," she whispered. "One that's made out of stone, and we'll have pretty words carved into it so everyone will know what a good pa you've been. As soon as Mary comes…"

Mary. She should have been here by now. What if she'd moved from San Francisco without telling Maggie or Pa? What if she hadn't received any of Maggie's letters? No, Maggie was being silly. Mary would do no such thing. If she'd even thought about moving, she would have told them first. Maggie's first letter might have been delayed, that's all.

She started to reverently smooth the dirt over the grave site, and grabbed a handful of rocks and strewed them over the area. She whispered an apology to Pa, and then tossed in some of the weeds and grass she'd pulled until the patch no longer looked like a grave. Sniffling, she pushed to her feet, and dusted her grubby hands together. It did little good.

"I love you, Pa," she murmured impulsively. "You never said the words, but I know you loved me, too."

She took a deep breath, and turned back toward the cabin. Not ten yards away, Cord stood watching her.

Their eyes met, his full of questions.

She swallowed convulsively, and foolishly tried to position herself between him and the grave. Had he heard her? "What are you doing out here?" she asked.

"I was concerned when you didn't come back."

She didn't know if she should abandon her post and lure

him back inside, or stay where she was and hope he hadn't seen the barren patch of ground behind her skirt. "Please, go." She made a shooing motion with her hands, but yanked them back when she saw how caked they were with dirt. She hid them in the folds of her skirt. "You were supposed to watch the bacon…it's going to burn."

"It's done and off the fire." His troubled gaze took in her dress, her horribly soiled dress. "You were gone a long time."

"I'm sorry. I, um…there was a lot to do in the barn." Slowly she walked toward him, mentally willing him to turn around and head back to the cabin. "Have you eaten? I can make more coffee. Or a pan of biscuits. It shouldn't take long."

He didn't move, even when she came to stand directly in front of him, for once, glad she was tall enough to block part of his view. "When did it happen?" he asked quietly, his eyes probing hers, searching for answers she didn't want to give.

Her heart hammered against her chest, and she lowered her lashes. "What?"

"He's dead, isn't he?"

The denial formed on her lips, but she didn't dare speak. If she uttered anything else, even the smallest sound, she feared she'd start sobbing. And that she simply couldn't bear. Reluctantly, she lifted her gaze, hoping he'd accept the small shake of her head.

The hard line of his mouth softened. Gold flecks warmed his eyes. "I'm sorry."

She swallowed around the lump in her throat, and then pushed past him. He had to follow her. What else could he do? Start digging to confirm his suspicion? Oh, God help her, he wouldn't dare. Yet what did she truly know of him, or his heathen customs?

If she made it to the cabin before him, she just might bolt the door. Let him find his way back to town. She didn't want him around anymore, with his knowing, concerned eyes. He was a stranger. An Indian, for heaven's sake. She didn't want his pity or sympathy. She wanted nothing from him.

Solitude. That's all she yearned for. The quiet that gave her thoughts free reign, allowed her fantasies to form and flourish. Allowed her to believe that in San Francisco, life could be different for a plain, common woman like herself. If only Mary would come.

And what if she didn't?

Maggie choked back a sob and ran the last few steps to the front porch. But before she made it to the door, Cord caught up and grabbed her none too gently by the arm.

"It's okay, Maggie. Me knowing about your father doesn't make a difference."

"Let go of me."

He loosened his hold, but she didn't believe that he'd allow her to escape inside. "Can you trust me a little more?"

She refused to look at him. "Why should I?"

"You said yourself, I've been a gentleman."

"Only because you think I'm plain." She covered her mouth with her dirty hand, appalled she'd spoken her thoughts aloud.

"What?" He sounded so startled that she glanced at him. His brows dipped in annoyance. "I never said that. For one thing, it isn't true." When she would've looked down, he hooked a finger under her chin and forced it up. "Maybe you shouldn't trust me, after all," he said, his warm gaze on her mouth.

"Why?" Her voice came out a pathetic squeak.

"Because I really want to kiss you."

Stunned, she didn't know what to say to that. She couldn't speak if she wanted to.

He smiled, and slowly slanted his mouth over hers.

Maggie held her breath, her hands fisting at her sides. Their lips touched and she automatically closed her eyes.

10

CORD LIGHTLY CUPPED her shoulders and smiled a little against her tightly seamed lips. Still, she didn't resist, so he moved his mouth to the corner of hers, touched the tip of his tongue there, and as soon as she relaxed, swept her lower lip and briefly drew the fleshiness between his teeth.

She stood ramrod-straight, her fascinated eyes slitted at first, and then when their gazes met, she squeezed them shut. He fully expected her to pull away but she didn't. Except she was so tense, her muscles taut under his palms, that he knew the experience wasn't entirely pleasant for her.

He drew back, letting his hands slide down the sides of her arms. Her eyes stayed closed, her cheeks as red as two ripe apples. "I'm sorry if that upset you."

She lifted her lids. Her eyes shining and moist, she slowly exhaled. "It didn't."

He moved a step away and released her hands when he realized he still held them. To his relief, she actually didn't look as upset as he'd expected. He couldn't explain his impulsiveness because he didn't understand the behavior himself. They'd finally found some safe footing. What a dumb-ass he was. "I don't blame you if you wanna kick me out."

"No." Her unsteady hand went to the tiny buttons of her high collar, her gaze going past him toward the road. "We'd better go inside in case we have any more visitors."

He didn't argue, but glanced over his shoulder before following her inside. She went straight for the coffee, poured herself a cup, grimacing as she gulped it through the steam, and then dumped water into the washbasin without giving him another look. Then her dismayed gaze went to the slab of bacon, which had gotten burnt around the edges, still sitting in the cooled skillet.

"What happened to your father?" he asked cautiously. "Was it illness that took him?"

She nodded jerkily. "I think his heart gave out. He'd been sick, but he wouldn't go see the doctor."

"I take it no one in town knows."

She drained her coffee, her face an unreadable mask. "I thought it wise they didn't, not until my sister gets here."

So that part was true. "When do you expect her?"

"Any day now."

He thought about the chest she had already packed. How long had it sat there waiting? "Isn't there a place in town where you could stay while you wait for her?"

"The hotel, but that costs money, and anyway, I wouldn't leave the cabin empty."

Cord frowned. It wasn't as if there was anything worth stealing. "I understand why you wouldn't want people to know you were out here alone, but you know this still isn't safe."

Her chin went up and her gaze went to the rifle leaning against the wall. "Like I said, I know how to use that Spencer carbine."

"You mean the unloaded Spencer carbine? Which you neglected to have on your person." He snorted. "No offense, but you'll recall, I had no trouble overpowering you."

She glared at him. "What do you care?"

He sighed. She had a point. "To tell you the truth, I don't know."

She set down the china cup with an annoyed clatter and picked up the basin. Water sloshed over the sides onto the floor as she hurriedly carried it toward the room. "I'm going to wash up," she murmured. "I'll see to finishing breakfast when I'm done."

"Maggie?"

She hesitated at the threshold, her back stiff, her gaze averted.

"About the kiss…"

She flinched.

"I won't do that again."

She gave a curt nod, and used the toe of her boot to push the door open wider.

"So, are we good?"

Turning slightly toward him, she wrinkled her nose.

It occurred to him that she didn't understand the phrase. "Do you want to skin me alive, or am I safe?"

"Both," she said, and slammed the door behind her.

MAGGIE SET DOWN the basin and quickly got to the business of unbuttoning her dress, anxious to be out of the soiled mess. She didn't bother to drag anything in front of the door. Cord wouldn't be pounding it down to get to her. He'd made that clear. Which was a great relief. Truly, it was. Especially now that he knew her pa wouldn't come rushing to her rescue.

But then he had the nerve to sermonize on her safety? What gave him the right? She had a good mind to make him walk to town. She fumbled with the buttons at her left cuff and noticed how badly the dirt had been ground into the blue fabric. If she ever got the stains out, it would be a miracle. Her hands and fingernails were dismally filthy, and she was appalled that she hadn't washed her hands before downing that cup of coffee.

She'd been rightfully punished, though. Her tongue and

lips still burned from the hot liquid. Or had it been the kiss that still made her tingle?

Angrily, she used a clean damp cloth to scrub her hands of most of the dirt and then she unfastened the stubborn cuff, popping off a button in her haste, and watched in dismay as it rolled beneath the cot. Sighing, she stooped to unhook her shoes, nearly falling over when she lost her balance. She gave in and sat on the edge of the cot to finish the task.

With her shoes safely set aside, she stepped out of the dress and then yanked off her petticoats, untied her muslin chemise and pulled down her drawers. Her annoyance with Cord and herself still simmering below the surface, she kicked aside the drawers carelessly, further irritated when she received insufficient satisfaction.

The air was chilly against her fevered skin and she belatedly noted that the bedroom window was open and the curtain indecently parted. She quickly crawled over the two cots still pushed together to get to the curtain, the action mimicking her earlier attempt to get away from Cord this morning.

The sudden and vivid recall of his bare bronzed chest seemed to suck the air from Maggie's lungs. Weak and exhausted suddenly, she curled up on the cot, drawing her knees tightly to her chest, and pulled up the quilt to cover her naked body. Even though she had little experience with the male form, she knew instinctively that Cord was different.

Land's sakes, even with his shirt on, the bulge of muscle along his upper arms and over his chest couldn't be hidden. Oh, how she'd longed to trail her fingers over his taut skin, explore the feel of smooth flesh pulled that firmly over sinew. The strangest thing of all, she noted, was how much more aware she was of her own body. Not because she was too tall or too thin. Lying next to him had done wonderful things to her insides. Odd sensations like being warm and comforted, and for the first time feeling as if she were a woman.

She touched the tip of one finger to her lips, remembering how he'd kissed her, wondering what her mouth had felt like beneath his. Unlike her callused hands, at least her lips were soft, really soft, like a rose petal. A newly picked rose like the ones they had in their garden back in Kansas, not like the bloom she'd long ago pressed between the pages of her bible. The hard, dried flower, she thought wryly, felt more like the palms of her hands.

But she wouldn't let that ruin her fantasy. She closed her eyes, and for the full effect, she pressed the length of two fingers across her lips and puckered, just a little, just the way Cord had when he'd kissed her. Though she couldn't seem to recreate the sensation. Surprisingly he'd used very slight pressure and hadn't scrunched his mouth up nearly as much as Clem had that day behind the old barn. Yet Cord's light kiss had awakened a yearning inside her she hadn't known existed until today. How could that be? How frustrating it was that Mary wasn't here to explain. Not that Maggie thought she'd have the courage to ask her sister something so terribly private.

She took a deep exasperated breath and her exposed nipple grazed the quilt. Her eyes flew open at the odd sensitivity. Curious, she touched the satiny crown with her forefinger. A pleasant shiver sluiced her spine. Daylight, and here she was naked as the day she was born, sprawled across her cot. Such wickedness would surely earn her no place in...

"Maggie?"

At the knock at the door, she stiffened and pulled the quilt more tightly to her breasts. "Wh-what do you want?"

Cord hesitated, almost as if he sensed the unspeakable things she'd been doing under the covers. Yet surely he could not. "Sorry to disturb you. If it's all right, I was going to put more bacon on to fry, maybe try my hand at some biscuits. But I didn't want to short you on your supplies."

She scrambled to the edge of the cot, the bulkiness of the quilt making her clumsy. "I'll be out in a minute."

"Take your time. Didn't mean to rush you."

"Help yourself to anything you want," she said, realizing she'd probably overreacted. That didn't stop her from hurrying to do her washing, while trying to keep the quilt partially wrapped around her body.

She tackled her upper torso first and then hastily donned a clean chemise while she finished up. Tonight she'd haul the tub inside, even wash her hair, but for now, she felt a great deal better with her hands and face scrubbed. It took her a while to get the drab brown dress buttoned—it had been passed down from Mary and the hem had been let out, but it was still two inches too short. Normally Maggie wore the dress only when she planned on staying around the farm.

Knowing she was a total fool for her vanity, since it wouldn't matter if she wore satin and lace—fabric wouldn't change her from plain Maggie—she stripped the dress off and pulled open the drawer to the small dresser tucked in the corner. Carefully wrapped in paper lay the pretty new pink checked dress she'd made special for the trip to San Francisco.

She'd been rather bold with the design, forgoing a high neck in favor of a modest scoop like a dress that she'd seen in a magazine. She reckoned that in a city like San Francisco it would be all right to expose part of her throat. Of course she'd only worn it once, just to try it on after she'd finished the row of tiny buttons up the bodice and the ruffle along the hem. To her best recollection, she'd owned only one other dress with a ruffle—one that Mary had made for Maggie's fifteenth birthday. Pa had been irritable over the extravagant use of fabric, but Mary had shushed him, like only Mary could.

Maggie smiled at the memory. She herself would never have dared talk back to Pa, but Mary had an authoritative way about her that even Pa had abided. Of his two married daughters, Maggie supposed Pa had missed Mary the most when she'd moved six years ago. Had Maggie had the good fortune to find a husband, would Pa have missed her? she wondered. She was the best cook of his three daughters, he'd always claimed, but it seemed they'd never had much to talk about, while he and Mary could make the weather sound interesting.

After she'd slipped on the new dress and fastened all the buttons, Maggie frowned at the snugness of the bodice. Yet how could that be? She'd made herself three dresses in the past two years, and had remained the same size. With the slight scoop, she should have more room. So was it her imagination? Or was it the sensitivity of her breasts making her bosom feel fuller? Or was the awkward fit punishment for touching herself wantonly? The thought made her cringe.

Refusing to dwell on such a notion, she quickly picked up her brush and ran it through her tangled hair. After fashioning a bun at her nape, she adjusted the bodice once more and, feeling reasonably sure that the snugness had been only her imagination, she opened the bedroom door.

Cord had just tossed a log into the fire, and he straightened, his gaze going directly to her bosom. The way his eyes darkened made her want to run and hide.

HE HADN'T MEANT to stare. Yet he couldn't seem to take his eyes off her as she swished past him in a rustle of skirts on her way to the kitchen. She had an extraordinarily tiny waist. How had he missed that before? And although she was slim, her hips flared out nicely and her breasts were high and well-rounded, again making her waist seem all the more narrow.

It struck him suddenly that he didn't personally know a single woman in L.A. who hadn't had some form of cosmetic surgery or another. Obviously, Maggie's attributes were all-natural. Unless she wore one of those corsets he'd seen in costume closets on the occasional movie set, but he didn't think so.

She turned around to find him still staring and gave him a disapproving frown before jerking her beige apron off a hook on the wall and tying the wide bands around her waist. "I see you know your way around a cookstove," she said, transferring her attention to the sizzling bacon and the pan of biscuits he'd attempted.

He shrugged. "My grandmother taught me some, but hunger was another great incentive."

"She teach you that fancy talk, too?"

"Right." He chuckled. "I barely got my GED," he said, without thinking, and when she frowned, he clarified, "Made it through high school."

She sent him a resentful look before focusing on the skillet and murmuring, "No need to make fun of me."

"No, Maggie. No." After being on the receiving end of taunting more times than he cared to recall, he'd be the last person to do that. "I come from a different sort of place. Very far from here. We go to school for a long period of time."

Her eyes lit up. "In a real schoolhouse?"

He smiled. "Yep."

"I went to one once back in Missouri," she said wistfully. "But that was a long time ago, before Mary started teaching Clara and me at home. I even thought I might want to be a teacher."

"Why didn't you?"

She blinked, clearly surprised. "Someone had to look after Pa. Besides, Mary is the smart one in the family. Brave, too," she added with obvious pride as she removed the skillet from the fire. "She didn't go so far as sassing Pa, but she wouldn't let him treat any of us like we had no brain at all. She'd be sure to remind him that all three of us girls could read and sign our names. Not in an unkind manner, mind you, because Pa never learned to do either."

"Hard to imagine you have a sister even smarter or braver than you," he said, and watched her eyes widen in disbelief.

"Mary was always the smart, brave one. And Clara, well, from the time she was thirteen, she was so pretty she couldn't stop heads from turning in her direction. Boys began courting her before she celebrated her fourteenth birthday. Pa used to get so riled at all those young men sniffing around that he swore he'd—" Maggie stopped, her cheeks turning that pretty pink. "Well, no matter, she found a nice husband by the time she marked her eighteenth year and has three young ones now, all of them cute as buttons. Although truth be told, I haven't seen the last one yet. Amy was born after they all moved back east." She got out two plates, her embarrassed gaze darting his way. "Listen to me prattle on. You must be starving."

An uneasy irritation climbed Cord's spine. Who had filled Maggie's head with that garbage about not being as good as her two sisters? He took the plates from her and set them on the small table. He should say nothing, he told himself. In a couple of hours he'd be out of her life for good. "Well, obviously I haven't met either of your sisters, but I don't believe either of them could be smarter, braver or prettier than you," he said casually. "How about more coffee?"

She stared at him, her green eyes wide, the color high on her cheeks, as if he'd just told her this horrendously far-fetched tale explaining that he was from the future and that he'd been sucked through time. "I'm not any of those things," she blurted. "I'm a very good cook. A good seamstress, too.

I'm not boasting. Pa said it all the time. About my cooking, anyhow." She blushed furiously. "Really, Mr. Braddock, you have the most annoying way of making a good Christian woman—" She waved a hand in exasperation.

He grinned. "Do what?"

She sighed, and set the skillet on the table. "Eat before this gets cold, too."

"Answer me something first." He moved around the table as if he were going to sit down, but caught her chin. "Does Clara have a cute upturned nose?"

She gazed at him with startled eyes, the green so clear and bright he could see his reflection. He felt her warm breath seep through her parted lips and bathe the base of his throat.

"Does she have eyes the color of the ocean at low tide right before it rushes back out to sea, or lips as pink and soft as brand-new rose petals? Does she?"

"Mr. Braddock, please," she pleaded softly, her head tilting back until he lost contact with her quivering chin.

"You're lucky I promised not to kiss you again, Maggie. And that I'm a man of my word." His gaze fell from her tempting mouth to the way her throat worked as she swallowed. "Instead, shall we talk about how brave you've been? How you faced me down, or how you've managed to live here on your own for weeks without any help? How you've outwitted the deputy and—"

"Please," she croaked out. "Don't." She grabbed the kitchen chair, leaned on it as if for balance, before pulling it out.

Oh, man. Was she going to faint again? He hadn't said anything out of line, and he hadn't kissed her. He just couldn't see her praising her sisters so damn much that she didn't recognize her own strengths. "I'm hungry. Thanks for breakfast," he uttered.

PLAY LUCKY 7 and get FREE Books!

HOW TO PLAY:

1. With a coin, carefully scratch off the silver area at the right. Then check the claim chart to see what we have for you—**2 FREE BOOKS** and **2 FREE GIFTS**—ALL YOURS FOR FREE!

2. Send back the card and you'll receive two brand-new Harlequin® Blaze™ novels. These books have a cover price of $4.99 each in the U.S. and $5.99 each in Canada, but they are yours to keep absolutely free.

3. There's no catch. You're under no obligation to buy anything. We charge nothing—ZERO—for your first shipment. And you don't have to make any minimum number of purchases—not even one!

4. The fact is, thousands of readers enjoy receiving books by mail from the Harlequin Reader Service. They enjoy the convenience of home delivery and they like getting the best new novels at discount prices, **BEFORE** they're available in stores.

5. We hope that after receiving your free books you'll want to remain a subscriber. But the choice is yours—to continue or cancel, anytime at all! So why not take us up on our invitation, with no risk of any kind. You'll be glad you did!

FREE GIFTS!
We can't tell you what they are... but we're sure you'll like them!

2 FREE GIFTS
when you accept our No-Risk offer!

Visit us online at www.ReaderService.com

NO COST!
NO OBLIGATION TO BUY!
NO PURCHASE REQUIRED!

➤ Detach card and mail today—No Stamp Needed ➤

Scratch off the silver area with a coin.
Then check below to see the gifts you get!

Slot Machine Game!

YES! I have scratched off the silver box above. Please send me the 2 free books and 2 free gifts for which I qualify. I understand I am under no obligation to purchase any books as explained on the opposite page.

351 HDL EW59   151 HDL EXAW

FIRST NAME   LAST NAME

ADDRESS

APT.#   CITY   HX-B-05/09

STATE/PROV.   ZIP/POSTAL CODE

7	7	7	Worth **TWO FREE BOOKS** plus **TWO FREE GIFTS!**
🍒	🍒	🍒	Worth **TWO FREE BOOKS!**
♣	♣	♣	Worth **ONE FREE BOOK!**
🔔	🔔	🍒	**TRY AGAIN!**

The Harlequin Reader Service—Here's how it works:

Accepting your 2 free books and 2 free mystery gifts (gifts valued at approximately $10.00) places you under no obligation to buy anything. You may keep the books and gifts and return the shipping statement marked "cancel." If you do not cancel, about a month later we'll send you 6 additional books and bill you just $4.24 each in the U.S. or $4.71 each in Canada. That is a savings of 15% off the cover price. It's quite a bargain! Shipping and handling is just 25¢ per book.* You may cancel at any time, but if you choose to continue, every month we'll send you 6 more books, which you may either purchase at the discount price or return to us and cancel your subscription.

*Terms and prices subject to change without notice. Prices do not include applicable taxes. Sales tax applicable in N.Y. Canadian residents will be charged applicable provincial taxes and GST. Offer not valid in Quebec. Credit or debit balances in a customer's account(s) may be offset by any other outstanding balance owed by or to the customer. Please allow 4 to 6 weeks for delivery. Offer available while quantities last.

"I'm a little hungry myself," she said, staring fixedly at her plate.

"Okay." He waited for her to sit and then took the other chair. "Let's eat. Then we'll talk about going to town."

"Oh, the biscuits." She wearily pushed back. "I forgot to check them."

"Stay where you are." He was up in a flash. "I'll go see if they're edible, but I'm not promising anything."

She gave him a faint smile, but then when he accidentally brushed her arm on the way to the stove, she shrunk away.

He was such an idiot. One step forward, two steps back.

He needed to give her space. It didn't matter that he'd be gone soon. Somehow it was important to him that they part on good terms.

Fortunately, the biscuits were turning a nice golden brown, and when he gave one a light poke, he was pleased to discover they wouldn't be breaking anyone's teeth.

"It's gonna be another five minutes for the biscuits," he said, bringing the coffee kettle back to the table with him. To his surprise, he noticed that she'd relaxed and a smile lurked at the corners of her mouth. "What?"

"I've never had a man cook for me before." She'd already cut the slab of bacon, taking a small piece for herself and setting a big hunk on his plate.

"After today, you may never want a man near your kitchen again." He poured coffee into her cup, and then topped off his before returning the kettle to the fire.

When he turned back to the table, he was startled to find Maggie right behind him. "I have something for you," she said solemnly and reached around him into a piece of brown pottery tucked behind the crock of sugar. "I've thought about this and I want the matter settled before we eat."

He heard the clink of coins before she withdrew her fisted

hand. Sensing what she was about to do, he drew back. "No, Maggie."

She nervously moistened her lips, and evenly met his gaze as she pried his fingers open. "I'll not take no for an answer."

11

"I CAN'T TAKE YOUR MONEY, Maggie. I won't." He firmly shook his head. "That's all there is to it."

She let out a groan of frustration when he refused to accept the coins, and then left her to go to the table. "I wish it could be more. I do. But it's all I have."

He picked up his fork and stabbed the hunk of bacon as if he wanted to punish it. Then he forked a big bite into his mouth and chewed intently.

She followed him to the table. "Your money won't be good in town. I've never seen the likes of it, and if I can't recognize those odd coins, do you think anyone there will take them?"

He slowed down his chewing, and his brows drew together in a harried frown. "Let me worry about that."

"Besides, trying to pass any of that off as legitimate money will only call attention to yourself."

"It is legitimate. It's just that—never mind." He took another angry bite.

"I'm just trying to help."

"You're low on sugar, coffee and flour. I suggest you use whatever you have in your hand to replenish your supplies. Bad enough you're sharing what you have with me." He stopped eating and stared at his plate, his mouth pulled into a grim line. "If you really wanna help, worry about yourself. You don't know when your sister will show up."

She sighed when she realized she'd hurt his pride. Should she tell him about the gold? She wouldn't have to tell him everything. Certainly not about how much she had stashed away. Or where Pa had found it.

"Then don't go into town at all. As I said, let me ask your questions for you," she said finally. "I know quite a few people. I could ask around at the general store. Even Mr. Carlson who sorts the mail seems to know everything that goes on. And Mr. Sherman at the barber shop. He's always been nice to me and says hello when I see him outside sweeping…."

One side of his mouth went up. "And if the trail leads you to the saloon? Or one of the whorehouses?"

She silently cursed the heat that climbed her neck. His observation hadn't been meant unkindly, but he had a point.

"You're the one who said I'm brave," she muttered. "If that's where the answers lead me, then…" She swallowed. "So be it."

He reached across the table and covered her hand with his much larger one. "You are brave, and I thank you for making the offer." He lapsed into silence, staring at her for a long thoughtful moment. "If it's okay with you, after I'm done in town, maybe I could come back here for another night."

Her heart leaped.

"It's been a while, but I used to be a pretty good hunter. Maybe I could catch some meat to help stretch your rations until your sister gets here."

"Oh. My goodness, I almost forgot about the jerked venison Pa stored with—" She caught herself just in time. "Some dried fruit and nuts." Even if she told him she had some gold, she wouldn't have to admit to how much. He was right. Her supplies were low. She'd have to take some gold in to trade at some point. He could help her with that because if she were to go to the assayer's office, all kinds of questions would be raised about Pa. But did she trust Cord enough?

"Good." He seemed genuinely relieved. "Out in the barn? I hope the food is wrapped well enough to keep out the critters."

She nodded, not wishing to discuss the true location. "But if you want to stay another night," she said quickly, her voice too breathless. "Well, of course you're welcome here." Embarrassment burned in her chest. Hastily, she added, "And fresh meat might be nice for a change."

He smiled. "Thanks. At least I know I won't end up sleeping in an alley behind a saloon."

"Oh, goodness no, you know there's a perfectly good cot—"

The memory of last night washed over her. The cots pushed together. His naked chest. She stared purposefully down at her plate, and was actually relieved at the first whiff of burning biscuits.

CORD MADE SURE there wasn't another soul in sight before he asked Maggie to stop the wagon about a quarter mile from the edge of town. She'd wanted to take him closer but he'd flatly refused. If things didn't go well in Deadwood, he didn't want her associated with him in any way. That's why he'd reconsidered about outright borrowing the wagon or using her father's horse. Besides, Floyd Dawson's handsome chestnut was recognizable enough that Cord didn't need to be accused of horse-stealing.

He'd conceded to her suggestion that he wear a hat. She didn't have to point out that his longish straight black hair would net him enough attention. If he'd been really smart he would've asked her to whack it off for him, but too much of the day had already slipped away.

"I don't understand why I shouldn't wait for you," Maggie began for the third time as he jumped off the wagon. "Do you know how long a walk it is back to the cabin?"

"About the same distance we just traveled, right?" He winked at her.

She rolled her eyes. "I hate leaving you here."

"I know." He came around to her side of the wagon, tempted to haul her down for a farewell kiss. He didn't know what he would find in town. The Winslow women? Possibly, even though he didn't think it would be that easy. But if he did happen to find them, if he found his way back to his own time, this was it, he wouldn't see Maggie again. He shouldn't care. He'd known her for only a little over twenty-four hours.

So why did he suddenly feel like crap? Why did he already miss the way her small straight white teeth nibbled her bottom lip when she was nervous, or how she blushed all the way to the roots of her pretty auburn hair?

She shaded her eyes so that she could see into his. Her eyes really got to him. From the beginning. Not just the color, which was a lovely hue of green he'd never seen before, but because they were so sweet and without guile. "Be careful."

"I will. I promise." He gave her a reassuring smile and picked up her hand. His gaze never wavered from hers as he pressed his lips to the back of her work-roughened knuckles.

"Oh, heavens, don't do that. They're awful." She tried to pull away, but he took her palm and pressed another kiss there.

He released her and said, "Now get before someone sees us together."

"I don't care. You might need—"

"Go," he said, before the pleading in her voice got to him. "I mean it."

Maybe he should've secured the reins from her and turned the wagon around himself. But he'd thought the argument was over, that she understood that he had no choice but to go into town. He explained his doubt that he'd be accused of attacking the stagecoach just because he was a half-breed. That would've been the first description of the bandit given to the sheriff. He didn't totally believe that, he knew how twisted bigotry and hatred was, but the reasoning had seemed to give her some peace of mind.

The best he could do now was take off for town and hope she came to her senses and went home. Against every urge, he didn't look back as he jogged toward Deadwood, straining to listen for signs that she'd started to wheel the wagon away.

Still, it was nice that she worried about him. The idea left a warm feeling in his chest. But he'd done the right thing. Bad enough he might never see her again, he didn't want to leave knowing he'd left her in harm's way. The only thing that bothered him now was walking around without suitable currency in his pocket. He couldn't even buy information if it came to that. Hell, he couldn't even afford a drink at the saloon. Maybe he'd be able to pick up an odd job. One of Deadwood's fine upstanding citizens may find that they could use some muscle.

The idea felt oddly uncomfortable, even though in the past year he'd hired himself out for less noble causes. He glanced at his watch. Solid gold. He could trade it, if push came to shove. The thought didn't rattle him as he would've expected. Better that than being some suit's thug. He'd hate for Maggie to find out that he'd strong-armed someone who hadn't paid a gambling debt, or worse.

He smiled when he recalled her asking where he'd learned his fancy talk. If she only knew he'd once had next to nothing, that without finding the Winslow sisters, he was a step away from returning to nothing again. His gaze went back to the pricey watch. The last symbol that he'd actually become someone. That he'd eaten the best food, drank the best wine, attended A-list parties with some of the most beautiful women in Hollywood at his side. By the time he got back…if he got back…he'd sort himself out, he thought grimly, and picked up his pace.

He didn't slow down until the stables at the edge of town came into view. A couple of kids played behind the livery but they were too intent on a game of tag to notice him approaching on foot. Still, he stayed off the road, hoping to remain inconspicuous until he could mingle with the early afternoon crowd swarming the boardwalk and spilling onto Main Street.

Just as it had yesterday, amazement filled him over the population of Deadwood. He might've expected a handful of women going from shop to shop, or a few horses tied to hitching posts outside the saloons and the general store, maybe the occasional cowboy coming out of the barber shop or bath house.

But the place buzzed with activity, from children playing on the street, to the groups of Chinese merchants who sold their wares from tents or paddled dirty laundry in huge bins of steaming water wedged down narrow alleys. Behind the hotel, they hung large sheets and towels to dry in the breeze, and from the chimney stack of Amos and Selma's Eating Establishment, the smell of roasting chicken wafted through the air.

He passed the newspaper office, a dress shop, the Gem Saloon and the telegraph office without anyone sparing him a glance. When he saw the sign for a hotel, he knew from Maggie's directions that he was close to the Golden Slipper. He stopped to gain his bearings and stared hard at the newer cream-colored building that looked somewhat familiar. Then it hit him. Where he'd seen the off-center door and second-floor balcony that seemed to come out of nowhere.

His heart slammed against his chest.

The old Winslow house. This was it. How it must have looked over a hundred and thirty years ago. Yeah, yesterday morning was the first time he'd laid eyes on the place but he was pretty sure he was right. He squinted up at the attic window, the same one he'd stared out of less than thirty hours ago. If he was right, he knew what he'd find when he turned around.

Sure enough, in the distance, a distinctive mountain peak jutted into the clear blue sky, looking like a piece of broken glass that someone had left behind. It was exactly how he remembered it. He slowly turned back toward the building, both excitement and dread surging through his veins. This house had to be the key. The attic. The chest. Had the sisters opened the same chest? Had they found the camera?

Through his jacket, he absently touched the two photos he had tucked in his breast pocket. A new thought started forming in his addled brain. Had that very camera been used to take the pictures of the two women?

"'Scuse me, mister," a man grumbled as he shouldered past Cord. "Hard for a body to pass when you're taking up the whole dang boardwalk."

Cord snapped out of his trance and looked dumbly at the portly man with the scraggly blond beard and missing teeth who'd passed him but glared over his shoulder. Others swirled around him as he'd stood gawking at the Winslow house, also known as the Golden Slipper.

"Go on in," another man said jovially. "Them ladies don't bite."

"The hell you say. A couple of them wildcats will take a whole chunk out of you," a third man chimed in to a gale of raucous laughter as a group crowded through the door of the brothel.

Cord pulled his hat lower and followed them inside the dimly lit room. The smell of stale tobacco, sour whiskey, cheap perfume and sex assaulted him like a blow to the gut. Already the place was nearly full, the customers mainly miners judging by their appearance. The sign over the bar that said No Bath, No Service was a joke. Cord had a strong stomach, but the place reeked with body odor.

The group that preceded him broke up with three of the

men heading for the bar, and the other two diving into the arms of a pair of petite voluptuous brunettes who could be sisters. Cord had already decided he was sticking with the Pinkerton cover story, but he wished the bartender wasn't so busy with half the stools at the bar taken.

Cord idly patted his pockets, wishing he had money for a drink. Just one that he could nurse at the bar to help him blend in while he waited for the bartender to get a free minute. Around here, a man who didn't take a drink was probably immediately suspect.

He frowned when he felt some coins in a pocket where none should be, and then dug in to produce a gold piece he didn't recognize. Several more jingled inside his jacket. He fished them all out. They were the ones Maggie had tried to give him earlier.

That sly little devil. He almost smiled, and then cringed under a crashing wave of guilt. Damn it. She couldn't afford to part with this money. He had to get it back to her. His gaze scanned the mahogany bar, the landscape prints on the red and gold velvety papered walls, his heart beating faster again with the knowledge that the key to his return to L.A. could be within reach.

"What's your pleasure, mister?" The barrel-chested bartender spoke to him over the head of a balding man dressed in a neatly tailored gray suit.

"Whiskey," Cord replied, belatedly wondering if beer wouldn't have been cheaper.

The bartender gave him an assessing look, and then nodded before reaching for a bottle of the amber liquid and pouring some into a shot glass. "I ain't seen you here before," he said, setting down the glass in front of an empty stool. "New to town?"

Cord took his cue and sat, glad for the opening. "Yep."

The man made no bones about eyeing Cord's well-tailored clothes. "From back east?"

"San Francisco," he said, deciding to stick as close to the truth as possible.

"Same thing, you ask me." The man's pale blue eyes narrowed. "Looks to me like you got some Indian blood in ya."

Cord lifted a brow. "That a problem?"

He shrugged his beefy shoulders. "Not to me. Them's pretty fancy duds you're wearing for your kind. Figured you got 'em made back east."

"Chester, quit your yappin' and get over here and fill my glass," someone yelled from the far end of the bar.

The older bartender muttered a curse that made his sagging jowls quiver and then grabbed the bottle of whiskey and waddled toward the complaining customer.

Cord swiveled around to survey the room filled with scantily clad women sitting with their horny customers on couches or groping each other in corners. He sensed that Chester's comment about him being Indian really had come from curiosity and not animosity, which could work in Cord's favor if he played his cards right. Everyone else in the smoky room had far lustier things on their minds than giving him information. The nosy bartender would be his best bet. Besides, he hadn't met a bartender yet who didn't know everything that was worth knowing.

Problem was, Cord might have to part with more of Maggie's money for a hefty tip. His gaze stopped on the gleaming gold watch circling his wrist. He knew what he had to do. Winter was coming and Maggie couldn't be sure her sister would come for her. Even if he found his way back to present-day L.A., how could he leave her penniless and defenseless?

He shook his head and downed the whiskey he'd fully intended to make last for the next twenty minutes. Chester returned as he set the empty glass on the bar and refilled it.

Just as it occurred to Cord that the man hadn't given him any change from the gold piece, the bartender laid some coins on the bar.

Cord arbitrarily chose one he thought looked like a half-dollar and slid it toward Chester.

"Thank you kindly, mister." The bartender quickly pocketed the tip. "You know which of the girls you want," he said, sliding a glance toward the staircase. "I can steer you right."

"Actually, I was hoping you could answer a few questions."

The man frowned. "Maybe. Maybe not."

"I'm looking for two women that went missing about a year ago." Cord slid a hand into his pocket, briefly wondering which of the two sets of photos he should be showing the man. The current ones he kept in his wallet, or the ones he found in the attic. He decided to start with the attic photos.

Chester squinted at the first one of Reese Winslow alone, the flicker of recognition that gleamed in his eyes making Cord's pulse quicken. "What's it to you?"

"I've been hired by their parents to find them."

The man's brows went up. "You one of them Pinkertons?"

"That's right."

Chester nodded, his jowls wobbling as his gaze roamed the cut of Cord's blazer. "Should've known right off." He stared at the picture a moment longer and then said, "Yeah, I seen her. Caused enough of a ruckus around here. Been a while though."

"What about this one?" Cord tried to stay cool as the sweat popped out on the back of his neck and he slid the second photo of Reese and Ellie together across the bar.

"Can't say for sure about the second one." His face creased in thought and he used the cuff of his shirtsleeve to mop his damp forehead. "She might've been the one with that gambler that showed up here about six months back. Yeah, that's right. They were asking questions about the runaway whore, too."

"The blonde? A whore?"

"Yep, showed up with the other two women Margaret had sent for from back east, except that one was wearing a wedding dress, if that don't beat all." The bartender chuckled. "And then she tried to pass herself off as a doctor."

Someone yelled for another beer, and Chester ambled off, leaving Cord suddenly so pumped with adrenaline he could scarcely keep from reaching across the bar and grabbing the man's shirt to keep him planted and talking.

Crazy thoughts swirled with alarming speed through his brain. The chatter and piano music behind him blurred to a static hum as his gaze tracked Chester, who was laughing with a lanky, ruddy-faced cowboy at the other end of the bar and now seemed to be in no hurry to get back.

Cord couldn't wait. He drained his second whiskey and then held up the empty glass. "Bartender."

Muttering along his way, Chester dutifully returned with the bottle. Before he finished pouring, Cord supplied him with another hefty tip, and asked, "Who's this Margaret you mentioned?"

Chester swept up the coin and glanced toward the top of the stairs at a hard-looking fortyish brunette. "Here she comes now. That, my friend, is Margaret Winslow. She owns the place."

12

"HOWDY, BOYS!" Margaret Winslow made her grand entrance as if she were holding court.

"You're up early, Margaret," a man called from the bar.

"That's because I heard you were down here, handsome." She tossed her dark head, sending a riot of upswept corkscrew curls bouncing about her dramatically painted face and earning a chorus of good-natured laughter.

Granted, she looked younger and prettier when she smiled, but Cord couldn't see any resemblance to either of the two sisters. Didn't matter. She was a Winslow, and now he knew he was on the right trail.

Her small dark eyes shrewdly swept the room, and she stopped to nod twice to two of her customers before her gaze came to rest on Cord.

The fleeting expression on her face told him he'd sparked her interest. Just as quickly though, her practiced features went blank. As she took her time descending the last few stairs, she carefully lifted her scarlet satin skirt to reveal a flash of cream-colored lace. Then she sashayed across the room, stopping briefly to fuss over the occasional string tie or pat an eager knee or whisper into the ear of an admirer.

But Cord knew without a doubt she was headed toward him. Good. Saved him the trouble of finagling an audience with her. He just hoped she was as amenable to answering his questions as Chester had been. Trying to tamp down his impatience, he picked up the photos off the bar and slid them into his pocket, knowing he'd have to wait for the right time to show them to her. He carefully wrapped his fingers around his shot of whiskey, sipping slowly, feeling the strong liquor slide down his throat like liquid fire and then pool in his churning gut.

"Afternoon, stranger," Margaret said, sliding up on the stool beside him, her cloying floral scent enough to gag him.

He silently cleared his throat. "I'm not all that strange." He turned and flashed her a slow grin. "Once you get to know me."

Her red-tinted mouth curved into an appreciative smile. "Well-spoken, well-dressed. My, oh, my." Her gaze ran down to his chest and lingered suggestively. "You're obviously not a prospector or a lawman or a cowboy. What brings you to Deadwood?"

"What makes you think I'm not a lawman?"

Her brows arched in surprise, a flicker of self-doubt in her dark eyes, and then she smiled again. "You couldn't afford this." She dragged a long red nail down his lapel.

"He's a Pinkerton," Chester stated. "Come here to ask questions about your runaway whore."

Cord mentally winced. Damn the man's timing.

Margaret's face pinched into a strained expression and she drew back, motioning for Chester to get her a drink. "That right?"

"I don't know if we're talking about the same woman." Cord shrugged casually. "The one I'm looking for isn't a whore."

"Short? Blond?"

"Show her the picture you got," Chester said as he set a small glass with some kind of red concoction in front of Margaret.

She slid the man a disapproving frown, and in a low threatening voice said, "I don't want to see any empty glasses on this bar."

His brows dipping, Chester didn't look happy with her tone, but he took the hint and disappeared.

She turned back to Cord. "Are we talking about a reward?" she asked, suddenly all business.

"Possibly. Her parents are the ones who hired me. Why? What do you know?"

She studied him for a moment. "I know she wasn't one of the women I contracted with, after all. My girl showed up on the stage three weeks later. Seems she'd been ailing and wasn't able to make the trip with the other two." She smiled thinly. "Too bad. That little blonde had them lining up in here waiting for her to get caught. That's why I've never been too anxious to set the record straight."

"You haven't told me where she went."

"Let's see that picture Chester was jawing about."

Cord handed over the one of Reese alone.

"Might be her," she said cagily. "Tell me about the reward."

Cord kept a poker face, even as he thought about how right at home Margaret would feel back in modern-day Hollywood. "What about this one? Have you seen her?"

Margaret examined the grainy photo of the two sisters. "I believe I have." She sipped her drink. "I should think that would fatten the reward pot."

"Only if you know where they are right now."

Her smile faltered, but not enough to dampen his hope. "What kind of money you offering if I send you in the right direction?"

"Tell me what you got and we'll see."

She laughed. "You probably already heard that she ran off with that livery man Sam Keegan."

He nodded, tried to look indifferent and hoped she couldn't hear his heart pounding. Another piece of the puzzle and damned if it wasn't starting to look as if he hadn't gone friggin' crazy after all. If the two sisters *had* traveled through time it meant he was closer to finding the way back.

"The old sheriff publicly accused him of horse-thieving, but Sam didn't steal any horse."

"You're not telling me anything I don't know, sweetheart." He took another sip of whiskey, doing his best to look bored.

Margaret snorted. "Aren't you the cocky one?"

He shrugged a shoulder. "You want to get paid for information, you have to give me something new."

She pensively pursed her red lips as if she were weighing her most advantageous move. Finally she said, "Doc knows something. Not the new one, but Doc Ballard. He's a friend of Sam Keegan's and he's been—"

Behind them, the shattering of glass followed by an anguished cry rose above the buzz of the crowd. The piano music abruptly stopped.

"I told you to keep your goddamn hands off her, you stupid bastard," a man challenged.

"Chester, the shotgun." Margaret had already slid off the stool and had turned to face the commotion with an angry swish of her satin skirt. "Sylvia, go get the sheriff," she ordered in a low voice to a wide-eyed young blond woman who'd come running to her side. "Everybody calm down. Tom, hand over that broken bottle right now. You know better than this, you stupid old fool," she said to the tall thin man with a drooping mustache, who was wielding an empty whiskey bottle and staggering toward a younger man cowering in the corner. "I won't have this in my place."

Cord hesitated long enough to watch her fearlessly enter the melee while everyone else froze in horror, and then he backed away from the bar and followed the woman named Sylvia out the door. He didn't want to be here when the sheriff arrived. It didn't matter that he hadn't been involved in the trouble. Old habits died hard. Besides, he'd learned enough from Margaret. She'd milk him for money if he let her, but he doubted she had anything more useful to add. Then, too, he could always come back if necessary.

Outside, the afternoon sun momentarily blinded him and he had to shoulder through the curious crowd that had gathered in front of the Golden Slipper's door. From the opposite side of Main Street, he saw a potbellied man running ahead of Sylvia, the sunlight gleaming off the tin star he wore on his chest.

Feigning deference to the chill, Cord lowered his head and hunched his shoulders, so that he wasn't so much taller than everyone else. He easily slipped through the crowd in the direction of the livery. He was pretty sure he'd seen the doctor's shingle hanging in front of a dilapidated older building across from the stables. Margaret had warned him that the new doctor wasn't the man to see, but who better than him to lead Cord to his predecessor.

He made it past a saloon and the barber shop when he thought he saw Maggie's wagon and old swaybacked mare by the general store. Then he saw Maggie, standing on the boardwalk, her face pale, a man clutching her arm.

"I DON'T SEE WHAT we have to talk about, Deputy," Maggie said with all the patience she could summon, clasping her purchase to her breast. She didn't really need the small sack of sugar, but had only wanted an excuse to go into the general store to ask questions for Cord and then give him a ride back to the cabin. "I already told you this morning that I will give Pa your message. Don't reckon I can do more than that."

"You were in town yesterday."

"Is there a law against coming to town two days in a row?" she asked sweetly, amazed at her boldness. No good could come of provoking the man, but that he seemed to be keeping track of her movements made her so angry that she truly wanted to slap his arrogant face. Against every ounce of good judgment she possessed, she'd stopped at the assayer's office not more than ten minutes ago to trade some of Pa's gold. And Lester probably knew all about the transaction by now.

Darn him. Darn her foolishness. She should have waited until next week or until the last of her supplies were gone. Mary could be here by tomorrow, and Maggie wouldn't have had to take the risk. But she'd given everything she had to Cord….

The deputy's insolent gaze went from the sack of sugar to her neckline, and for a reckless moment, she wasn't sure she could keep her hand from striking out. "That's a mighty pretty dress you're wearing. I don't believe I've seen it before."

"Why, Deputy, I didn't know that you kept up with what the women of Deadwood have been wearing."

His beady-eyed gaze raised to meet hers in a challenge. "We've known each other a while now, Maggie," he said, emphasizing her name. "How about you call me Lester? In fact, how about you stay and have some supper with me at the hotel?"

Staring into those cunning depths, she realized at that precise moment that Lester knew she'd brought in the gold. Besides, there was only one reason he'd suddenly invite her to supper. He wanted something from her. Icy fear chilled her to the bone. Did he know about Pa, too? Why he'd been unable to do the trading as he'd done for the past two years? Would she ever be safe at the cabin alone again?

"That's not possible," she said, trying to keep her voice even and pleasant as she hurried away from him. "But I thank you kindly for the invitation."

"I'm not done talking to you." His hand snaked out and he grabbed her arm. This time his grip was frighteningly painful. "You best be more—"

"Maggie."

At the sound of Cord's voice, she turned her head. He was crossing Main Street and headed straight for them. When she saw the deadly glint in his eyes, relief slid into panic. Someone was about to get hurt. She tried to shake free of Lester, but he seemed transfixed on the sight of Cord bearing down on them.

"Deputy," she pleaded with a jerk of her arm.

Cord stepped up on the boardwalk, his angry gaze fastened to the deputy's hand. "I'll give you one second to release her."

Lester let her go, but reached for his side iron. "Who in the hell—?"

Cord caught the deputy's wrist before he could so much as graze the butt of his gun, and twisted the man's arm up behind his back. "You're even stupider than you look."

At the deputy's howl of pain, followed by a vicious curse, people scattered from the boardwalk.

"Stop it!" Maggie tugged at Cord's arm. "Both of you."

Cord sent her a resentful look, and she gave him a beseeching one back.

Lester tried unsuccessfully to pull away. "You're gonna break my fucking arm."

Cord abruptly let him go, and the man fell backward against the general store window. "If you're thinking about going for that gun, I'd think again."

Embarrassment and fury merged in the deputy's face, but he kept his hand lowered.

Maggie got between them, and artfully rubbed her upper arm. "You *were* hurting me, Deputy." She scrambled for the right thing to say. "What did you expect my cousin to do?" It was the best she could come up with.

Both men looked at her. Fortunately, Lester didn't see that Cord was as shocked as he was.

"Your cousin?" Lester turned to peer more closely at Cord, and with pure loathing said, "You got Indian blood in you."

Maggie promptly linked an arm with Cord's, hoping to forestall him from punching the lawman. Not that she wouldn't delight in seeing Lester with a broken nose, but she didn't want Cord to end up in jail. "He's related on my mother's side. I'm done here. How about you?" she asked Cord with a bright smile and pointed look.

For a moment, he didn't seem interested in supporting her blatant lie, and then he gave a curt nod.

"Where are you staying?" The deputy clearly didn't know when to shut up. Maybe she should let Cord punch him. Especially when his expression turned to one of accusation. "With Maggie?"

She fought against the heat climbing her neck, struggled to find the right words, the right tone of voice to silence him.

"You got trouble over at the Golden Slipper," Cord interjected, his voice admirably calm. "Your sheriff is over there now trying to break up a fight."

He guided Maggie the few feet toward her wagon, giving Lester his back. But she saw the hard set of Cord's jaw, felt the coiled tension in his arm, and she sensed that without even a backward glance, Cord was fully aware of whether the deputy had even blinked. If Lester made a sudden move it would be over for the smaller man. She prayed they got out of town without further incident.

Her prayer was swiftly answered by Josiah Smith running toward them, shouting for Lester. "Come quick to the Golden Slipper," the young man called excitedly. "The sheriff needs you to haul one of the prospectors off to jail."

Lester muttered a vivid curse, and she heard the two men run off, presumably in the direction of the whorehouse.

"Your cousin?" Cord murmured as he helped her to the wagon.

His warm breath next to her ear started a fluttery feeling

in her belly. He grasped her waist and lifted her, as if she weighed absolutely nothing, onto the wagon seat. Never had a man done that before. At her height, most men would be unable to accomplish such a feat.

She didn't miss the stares, some curious, some surprised, some disapproving. To her amazement, she cared not a wit about any of them. She was content knowing that Cord was safe and that he was climbing up on the wagon beside her, and that they were on their way back to the cabin.

"What was that about?" he asked, taking the reins from her. When she didn't answer right away, he looked at her. "With the deputy."

"It's not that I don't appreciate what you did, but you shouldn't have interfered," she said, stalling, unsure how much to tell him about the gold, yet meaning what she said. "You don't need him as an enemy."

Cord furrowed his brow as if he didn't understand. "He was *touching* you. What else could I do?"

She swallowed at the slightly possessive indignation in his voice. The idea shouldn't thrill her so much. He meant nothing by the casual comment, she was quite certain, but it sounded so deliciously chivalrous, like something a hero might say in a dime novel. Not trusting herself to speak, she stared straight ahead, her hands tightly clasped in her lap.

"I'm sorry," he said gruffly. "I thought I was helping."

She realized he misunderstood her silence for sullenness, and she impulsively laid a hand on his arm. Even his forearm was taut with muscle, and her breathing faltered. She nearly snatched her hand back, but she liked touching him, liked the feel of the way his muscles rippled when he flicked the reins.

He cocked an expectant brow at her.

Reluctantly she withdrew her hand. "I'm grateful. He was

being a brute, and frankly, I'm not sure what I would have done. I was seriously close to slapping him."

Cord laughed. "I wish I'd known. I would've liked to have seen that."

She laughed, too, and then tried to cover up the sound with a cough. "You're terrible."

"Why? The guy deserved more than a slap."

"Yes," she agreed. "But he could cause trouble for me."

Cord's lips drew into a grim line. "Let him try and show his face at the cabin."

"You might not be there to protect me," she reminded him quietly.

His face grew impossibly more somber and after a stretch of silence he said, "I still have two more stops to make."

"Where?"

"The doctor's office, for one. Just up ahead on the right, isn't it?"

"He's not there. He's delivering a baby a few miles north of town. Besides, he's not the person you want to talk to."

Cord turned his head to stare questioningly at her.

"I did some poking around myself," she told him, uncomfortable suddenly, hoping he didn't think her nosy. "I asked at the general store about the women you're looking for. It seems one of them was a friend of Doc Ballard's, the old doctor we had."

He nodded. "I heard about him."

"Well, he's gone and I don't expect the new doc knows where, but according to Mr. Carlson, our postmaster, Doc Ballard had taken several trips before eventually disappearing. Each time he bought supplies for about a fifty-mile trip."

"Meaning?"

She shrugged. "The road heads north to Leed or south to Hay Camp. He could've gone in either direction."

Cord thought about what she'd said in silence, and then asked, "Who's the person that converts gold to money in this town?"

"You mean, Mr. McGreevy?" She reared her head back, her heart thumping. "Why?"

"What's he called?"

"An assayer?" she said slowly. This was a mining town for heaven's sake. Everyone knew what an assayer was. Why was Cord being so odd? And why on earth did he need an assayer? Had he seen her slip into Mr. McGreevy's office earlier? Was this Cord's way of getting her to talk about the gold? "Why do you want to know about Mr. McGreevy?" she insisted.

"Where's his office?"

"You have gold to trade?"

"Something like that."

She didn't understand the hesitancy in his voice or his apparent reluctance to look at her. "His office is closed today."

"Ah." Oblivious to her lie, he seemed genuinely disappointed so she quickly dismissed the idea that he'd seen her visit the assayer's office earlier. "Open tomorrow?"

"I'd assume so." She fidgeted, sorry now that she'd lied. But she was still curious. "Of course it's none of my business…"

He shrugged a shoulder, nudged his chin toward his wrist. "This watch is solid gold. It should get us a decent price."

Her gaze fell to the timepiece. Naturally she'd noticed it, only peripherally, but for the first time she really looked at the stunning craftsmanship, the likes of which she'd never seen. "It's beautiful," she whispered. "Why would you trade it?"

His lips lifted in a sad smile. "You gave me the last of your coins, Maggie. And fine as this watch might be, sitting on my wrist won't help fill your empty belly."

13

HE'D BEEN WILLING to sell his fine gold watch to keep her fed this winter. Even two hours later while fixing supper, Maggie couldn't think of the enormity of his generosity without swallowing back a lump of emotion. Without question she would never allow him to do such a thing. Even if she had to confess about the hidden gold that would keep her comfortable for a very long time, probably forever. But she couldn't tell him yet. It was still too difficult to speak.

With astounding clarity, she knew that tonight she would lie with him. Do all the things a man and woman did on their wedding night. Not that she was certain what that entailed exactly. She had a broad suspicion, but she'd never actually discussed the particulars with either of her sisters. And since their mama had died when Maggie was so young, there really hadn't been anyone else to go to for information.

She stared at her hands as she put the beans on to simmer. Surprisingly, she felt calm and steady, which had to mean her decision was the right one. After all, at twenty-five what were her prospects of meeting and marrying a nice fellow? Even if she weren't so tall and thin with unbecoming red hair, she wasn't aware of men courting women at her age. Although maybe in a big city like San Francisco, things were different.

Sighing, she nibbled at her lower lip as she pondered that possibility. Was she being foolish? Slanting a look at Cord, who was crouching to stoke the fire, her brief misgiving dissolved. The simplest thing, like his shirt straining across his broad shoulders and muscled back, made her skin tingle. Heavens, but even the way his straight hair defiantly waved a bit at the ends and touched his collar left her body feeling as though it belonged to someone else entirely.

She didn't recognize the physical reactions she was having. Well, maybe the breathlessness when Cord brushed her hand or shoulder. Still, she'd never experienced anything close to the scorching heat that she felt in his presence, or the repeated fluttering that started low in her tummy and blossomed torturously in her bosom. Maybe she was taking ill and didn't realize it.

A nervous laugh softly breached her lips. At the sound, Cord turned to look at her. His mouth curved in an earthy smile, almost as if he could read her thoughts. Absurd, of course, but even the threat that he might indeed know what she was thinking didn't stop her telling reaction to him.

No, her decision to lie with him would stand. It would be no mistake. The true folly would be to risk never knowing the pleasure of a man's touch. Of Cord's touch. The problem now was figuring out how she could give him a sign without acting like a shameless hussy.

She smiled back at him, her face so tense she thought it might crack. She tried to take a soothing breath but the attempt only made her chest hurt. How on earth was this going to work?

"You need some help?" he asked, rising easily to his feet and dusting his hands together.

"Maybe you could get some water?"

"Consider it done." He closed the space between them, casually brushing her arm as he reached around her to grab the bucket.

She nearly jumped out of her boots. He didn't seem to

notice, just strode out the front door without bothering to pull on his jacket. She hurried to the window to watch him eat up the distance to the well in that long easy gait of his. Too little sleep, too little food, too much worry over the past few weeks had stretched her nerves as thin as the threadbare kitchen towel hanging near the cookstove to dry.

Maybe she'd been wrong to turn down his offer of catching a rabbit for their supper. Maybe she needed the time alone so that she could think straight. Plan her seduction. The thought alone sounded so wicked she flinched. She wasn't sure she could even manage a minor flirtation. She envied his ease at casual touches, while she felt like a bull in Gladys Kent's millinery shop.

Naturally, she wasn't a temptation to him the way he was to her, so naturally that made it easier for him. The depressing thought made her rethink her position. What if she threw herself at him and he rebuffed her? How humiliating would that be? Then he'd leave, and she'd never see him again.

When he turned back toward the cabin, she quickly ducked away from the window and went back to stirring the pot of beans. She knew he at least liked her, but perhaps only as he would a younger sister. No, he'd kissed her. That had to mean something.

Well, she wasn't getting any younger standing here wasting her energy thinking on what to do. She had to act. And she would, heaven help her. Right after supper.

CORD REALIZED too late that he should've grabbed the rifle and gone after a rabbit to roast over the fire. The beans smelled great, and Maggie had brought out some cured ham she'd been saving, but food or hunger had almost nothing to do with his need to hunt. What he really longed for was fresh air, a cooling-off period. He needed to subdue the unwanted, unfamiliar feelings she stirred inside of him.

The lust was easy to identify and label, he thought ruefully as he watched her untie the apron from her small waist, her breasts jutting out as she reached behind to pull the big bow free. Tendrils of hair had escaped her bun and fell in long loose curls to her shoulders. His fingers itched to pluck the pins from her hair, let the weight of it fall down her slender back. Kiss a trail down her spine all the way to the sweet curve of her backside.

Unfortunately, that's not all he itched to do. He wanted to spread her thighs and plant himself so hard that her eyes would darken with need and her cheeks would turn that pretty pink, and she'd pant his name over and over again. The urge to brand her was so primitive it shocked the hell out of him. The slow simmer in his veins had started as soon as he'd seen the deputy lay his hands on her.

It was crazy because he'd never been the possessive or jealous type. Maybe because women had always been plentiful, or maybe because he hadn't cared enough about any one woman in particular. No, not true, he might have gotten serious about Dana if he hadn't been so young and her so starry-eyed over the whole Hollywood scene. But it was the sudden rage that erupted inside when he saw the deputy handle Maggie that astonished him.

Maybe it wasn't jealousy, but simply protectiveness. Although that alone confused him, too. He didn't like to see a lady hurt or uncomfortable, but he'd never been the chivalrous type, either. Then again, most of the women of his acquaintance back in L.A. were hardly the kind who needed protecting.

Cord pulled out one of the kitchen chairs and sat down. Building the fire had been a welcome distraction but he knew now he'd gone overboard. The flames spit and crackled, and blazing heat seared his back, even from several yards away.

He unbuttoned his cuffs, wishing he could lose the shirt altogether, but he didn't think Maggie would approve.

He settled for rolling up his sleeves. She came to the table carrying the pot of beans, her eyes widening slightly on his bared forearms.

"It's gotten warm in here," he muttered.

She smiled nervously, glancing at the roaring fire. "We'll need to open a window or two."

"Got it." He jumped up, glad for something to do.

"I hope you don't mind leftover breakfast biscuits."

"The beans would've been enough. They smell so good I—" He saw her unfasten the top two buttons at her neckline and lost his train of thought.

Her fingers fumbled, her gaze lowered to the table.

"I wish you hadn't brought out the ham, Maggie," he said, regaining his composure and reclaiming his seat. It wasn't as if he could see a damn thing. She probably had on a hundred layers of clothing under the dress. But the act of Maggie unbuttoning anything caught him off guard.

"You scarcely had anything to eat all day," she said, dropping her cloth napkin onto her lap and avoiding his eyes.

"You need to better ration your food," he cautioned, sounding more gruff than he'd intended. "What if your sister doesn't show up?"

She looked up then, fear flickering in her eyes before she blinked, and then she calmly picked up the knife and started slicing the ham. "I have faith that she will."

"Shouldn't she have at least responded to your letter by now?"

"I thought she would have." She placed a thick slice of ham on his plate. "Now, I'd prefer not to ruin our supper with such talk."

Fine. None of his concern. He waited for her to ladle some beans onto his plate and then for her to serve herself before he picked up his fork. When she bowed her head, he remembered grace, and laid his fork back down until she'd said her words of thanks.

What he really wanted to do was tell her to skip the gratitude and pray for her sister's arrival. Maggie's situation was bad enough before today, but now that the deputy had caught her in his sights, the man wasn't likely to back off. As soon as he knew Cord was gone…

Shit. He couldn't worry about that. Maggie had done fine on her own, and she'd have to take care of herself again. She didn't expect Cord to hang around. She knew he was here on a job, and that he'd have to leave as soon as he found the sisters. Even if he didn't find the Winslow women, he *had* to leave. He didn't belong here.

He had the sudden urge to tell Maggie about L.A., about the weird camera, the flash of light, the earthquake, the whole ridiculous series of events that had led him here. She wouldn't believe a word of it. Certainly she wouldn't understand. She'd think he was crazy. So he kept his mouth shut. Like she said, she didn't want to ruin supper.

"More beans?"

He looked down at his near empty plate. He was so preoccupied, he'd barely tasted the food. "This is really good. Thank you."

She beamed when he extended his plate for a second helping. Along with a mound of beans, she added another slice of ham.

Guilt gnawed at him. "Tomorrow I'll see how much cash this watch will bring. It's pretty heavy, all gold."

"No." The pleasure vanished from her face. "That's not necessary."

"I know, but I—"

"I have gold." Their eyes met briefly, before she stared down at her plate. "Money, too."

"You gave me everything you had, remember?"

She nodded. "Everything I had in the cookie jar. I have more."

Cord sighed. He hadn't meant to hurt her pride. He was just looking out for her. Didn't she understand that? "Look, I owe you a debt. You don't expect to get your goods for free at the general store, do you?"

She glared at him, picked her napkin up from her lap and threw it down on the table. "Do I look like a general store?"

Cord stared back, caught off guard. "All I'm saying—"

"Honestly, you can be so infuriating." She got up and picked up both their plates even though he hadn't yet started in on his second helping.

"I guess we're finished, huh?"

She stared blankly at him, and then noticed his full plate. She returned it to the place in front of him, and then with pursed lips, carried hers to the kitchen.

At a loss, he shook his head. "What did I say?"

She leaned over to scrape the leftover food from her plate into a pail, and his gaze followed the curve of her backside. He didn't know if it was his imagination or the way she was angled, but he could swear she wore one fewer layer of clothing. Maybe that was the trick, get the fire going so hot that she'd start peeling off clothes in self-defense.

She straightened and glanced at him before he could look away. Since she'd caught him red-handed, he unapologetically met her eyes. Her lips parted, but whatever she'd planned on saying never made it into words. She blinked, stared down at the plate, then squared her shoulders and slowly set it aside.

"Sit with me?" he asked quietly. "Whatever I said to make you mad I promise never to say again."

She shook her head and rolled her eyes.

"Maggie."

She sighed, and walked back to the table. Before she could

sit, he caught her hand and tugged her toward him, pushing out his chair to make room for her on his lap. She regarded him with wide, shocked eyes but she didn't resist as he pulled her closer, so close that he saw the erratic tic of the pulse at her throat. Her breasts rose with the breath she sucked in and seemed to hold.

Even before her curvy bottom made contact with his thighs, desire hit him so hard and fast that his stomach lurched. He had no idea what he'd intended when he'd drawn her toward him, but not that. He'd made a promise not to kiss her again, and he'd do his best to honor that vow, but if she gave him the slightest indication she might be interested… well…he was no saint.

He touched her face with the tips of his fingers, traced her lower lip with the pad of his thumb. "I knew your skin would be this soft."

She didn't move, not a single muscle. In fact, she was so rigid, he knew he'd made a mistake. "As soft as other women?" she whispered.

"Softer than most," he answered, trying not to let his surprise show.

"Really?" She lifted a hand and touched her cheek, a pleased look lighting her eyes. "Can I—" The tip of her tongue darted out and she hesitantly moistened her lips.

"What, Maggie? Go ahead."

"Can I touch you?"

He smiled. "Anytime, anyplace."

She pressed her lips together, flushing slightly before tentatively pressing her fingers to his stubbly chin.

"I know. I need a shave."

"I like the way you feel." She self-consciously shrugged a shoulder. "I've never been this close to a man before."

Her admission was like a dousing of cold water. Nothing

he hadn't begun to suspect but the reminder made him feel like the worst kind of jerk. Maybe his attraction to her boiled down to knowing in his bones that she was off-limits.

"Look, Maggie, I haven't forgotten my promise to you." He had to get her off his lap before he did something he'd regret, like ripping off the row of tiny buttons down the front of her dress with his teeth. Something he was dangerously close to doing. If she had any experience at all, she'd recognize the source of the bulge she was sitting on. That would be enough to scare her off.

Instead, she shifted her weight, and he gritted his teeth against the torturous pressure. "What promise?"

"Not to kiss you again."

"Oh." She pressed a tentative hand to his chest. "What if—" She noisily cleared her throat. "What if I said you didn't need to keep that promise?"

"You have to be more specific than that." He ran his palm soothingly down her back, which was knotted with tension on either side of her spine.

"I want you to—" She briefly closed her eyes. "I think I want you to kiss me again."

"Ah, Maggie, sweet, sweet, Maggie." He worked on the coiled muscles. "It's more complicated than that."

She wouldn't relax and, in fact, she stiffened even more. "What is?"

"Kissing you."

"Because you don't want to anymore," she said, looking so crestfallen that he almost grinned.

But he didn't want her to get the wrong idea and think he was making fun of her. Trying to conceal his amusement, he averted his eyes and nuzzled her neck. "Oh, no, I want very much to kiss you," he murmured against her rose-hued skin.

She shivered. "Then I don't understand."

He'd only served to torture himself further. She was so soft and she smelled so sweet. How was he supposed to walk away without a taste? Yet he knew better, damn it. She might not, but he did. "What if it's too hard to stop after one kiss?" he asked hoarsely.

"Oh." She sounded pleased and quickly relaxed against him. "Then we'll kiss again."

The slight weight of her warm body pressed to his arousal was almost more than he could stand. She didn't seem to notice the physical reactions she was causing. Was she really that clueless? If he had a shred of decency he'd shove her off his lap right now. She'd be upset at first, probably offended and confused, but in the long run, it was the kindest thing he could do for her.

"Maggie." His voice sounded strained to his own ears, and probably to hers because she looked at him strangely. "Maggie," he started again, "there are other things besides kissing that a man and woman do."

The red was back in her cheeks, the shock in her eyes, the starch in her spine as she pulled away. "I know that."

All he had to do was release her. She'd jump up and run to the kitchen, give him her back until the awkwardness passed. She'd clean up, while her embarrassment faded, and he'd tend to the fire until he wasn't so frustrated that he wanted to punch a wall. They'd both pretend nothing had happened. Everything between them would be normal by bedtime.

The pain in her eyes was like an arrow straight to his heart. He gathered her close again, waited while she struggled in the circle of his arms. "I'm not going to hurt you," he promised, his lips pressed to the side of her neck. "I just want to explain."

"Let me go," she whispered, her plea undermined by the way she leaned into him, her right breast pillowing his chest. She turned her face so that her lips brushed his temple.

"Is that what you really want?"

She hesitated, and he inhaled deeply, waiting for her response. One word from her and he'd be off the hook. He wouldn't have to feel like a jerk for appearing to have rejected her. She wouldn't understand how badly he wanted her or how much resisting her was costing him.

Ah, hell. What was wrong with him? He could kiss her. Satisfy her curiosity. Then stop right there. He wasn't an animal without self-control. Besides, kissing would probably be enough to scare the hell out of her. She was an innocent and a lady, and a lady guarded her virtue. Was he really that full of himself he couldn't see that he wasn't that irresistible?

"Time's up," he said, using a hooked finger to lift her chin.

She froze and lowered her lashes as his mouth covered hers. He kept the kiss light but her sigh of longing was nearly his undoing. When he parted her lips with his tongue, she didn't retreat as he expected, as he'd half hoped she would, but moved closer, opening for him with a tentative eagerness that shook him to the core.

Her palm moved to his chest, shyly touched his hardened nipple through his shirt. Cord tensed, ordered himself to take it easy and then, throwing caution to the wind, kissed her savagely, slanting his mouth across hers and molding his hand over her hip and backside.

Maggie whimpered but didn't fight him. She clutched his shoulder, digging into that tender spot near his scar and arching her back in silent invitation, and sorely tempting his nobility. It was up to him to stop, to put an end to this reck-lessness before it was too late. He would leave, and she'd be left behind, considered nothing more than damaged goods. God help him, if he ever needed to do the honorable thing, it was now.

14

MAGGIE STRUGGLED between nervousness and a warm syrupy feeling she couldn't put a name to. Her fevered skin tingled beneath Cord's lips and the growing dampness between her thighs both terrified and baffled her. Did he know what was happening to her? She was sitting on his lap, for heaven's sake. Yet he'd warned her. He'd told her there could be more than kissing....

He took her earlobe between his teeth and nibbled lightly before trailing his lips down the side of her neck and across her collarbone to the neckline of her dress. She squeezed her eyes closed, mortified over where his mouth was headed, but then quickly opened them again, more frightened of what he might do when she wasn't watching.

Not that she wanted him to stop. Though she couldn't explain why she trusted him. Trusted fully that he wouldn't hurt her. But when he took one of her bodice buttons between his teeth, she sucked in a tense breath. His arms tightened around her, and she felt one hand cup her backside and squeeze lightly. She stiffened, unwittingly pushing her breasts into his face.

He made a soft growling sound that vibrated against her sensitive flesh and heated a fluttery path all the way down to the pit of her stomach. His tongue darted out to toy with the buttons and dampened the fabric at her neckline, while his stubbly chin grazed her skin.

"Tell me to stop, Maggie, and I will," he whispered gruffly. "Just say it."

She moistened her parched lips. Shame and reason hovered along the fringes of her mind, but she stubbornly kept silent. Her only regret was that she didn't know what to do, how to respond or please him.

He stopped suddenly, and pulled back to look at her. His hazel eyes had turned a dark glassy brown and a sheen of sweat glistened on his brow. "Do you understand what I'm saying?"

She nodded jerkily, wishing she understood exactly what was happening, what she was expected to do next. She wanted to touch him as easily as he touched her. Without her hand shaking, without worrying that she would offend him or embarrass herself.

Cord loosened his arm around her. When he brought up his hand, she jumped. His mouth curved in a wry smile as he brushed the hair away from her face. Only then did she discover that her bun had come free, that her unruly hair hung down her back in a mass of tangles. He leaned toward her and gently kissed her mouth.

Too gently.

Her heart sank. In that instant, he'd changed, everything changed, the air between them no longer crackled with excitement. Was it her hair? Was it because she looked a fright? She quickly pulled her hair back to her nape, feeling for her hairpins.

"Don't, Maggie." He covered both her hands with his larger one. "Leave it down. Your hair is too pretty to be all tied up."

She swallowed, her mind racing, searching for the right thing to do. Ineptly, she leaned toward him and their lips met clumsily. She felt his weak smile against her inexperienced mouth and, awash with embarrassment, she wished she could die on the spot.

"I'm sorry," she said feebly, keeping her gaze downward as she drew back from him.

He feathered his thumb across her quivering lower lip. "I'm the one who needs to apologize. I knew better."

Confused, she was tempted to look up then, seek an explanation in his face. But she couldn't bring herself to meet his eyes. If she saw one ounce of pity there, she could never look at him again.

He moved suddenly, grasping her by the waist and setting her on her feet before she knew what had happened. Startled by the abruptness of his actions, her gaze automatically went to his face. He smiled at her with such gentle understanding she wanted to weep.

She could have taken just about anything else but kindness. Damn him to—

That she'd sworn, even silently, shocked her to the tips of her toes. Apparently, Cord was responsible for making her do a lot of things she'd never before considered. She lifted the hem of her skirt high off the floor, because the last thing she needed was suffering the indignity of tripping and falling flat on her face, and spun away from him.

"Maggie, wait."

As she headed for the washbasin, she grabbed her long curly hair and wound it tighter than a miser's fist. She could only find one hairpin in her mass of tangles, since she would not stoop to look for the others that he'd discarded when she'd been too caught up in his web. The thought of what she'd been about to allow him—no, not just allow but had yearned for him to do—made fresh shame burn behind her eyes.

"You deserve better, Maggie," he said so softly that she nearly didn't hear him before he turned away.

She blinked away the threatening tears, her chest suddenly tight with emotion. Did his stopping have nothing to do with her inexperience, after all? She forced herself to breathe in deeply and slid a look at his retreating form.

He disappeared into the bedroom, and she exhaled with a whoosh of air. A moment later he emerged carrying one of the cots. Disappointed, she watched him set it up near the fireplace. Somehow she knew she should be grateful. But she wasn't. Not in the least.

"WHERE THE HELL have you been, Lester?" Ernest McGreevy bellowed through the haze of smoke as he leaned back in his office chair, straining the buttons of his tailor-made shirt and puffing on his expensive cigar. "The girl left hours ago."

"There was a ruckus at the Golden Slipper and the sheriff needed me." Lester didn't like McGreevy. The arrogant son of a bitch was nothing but a loudmouthed snake in the grass who'd cheat his mother out of her egg money if he thought he could get away with it. But he paid Lester well to do his dirty work, a lot more than what Lester made wearing that lousy tin star and getting shot at by drunk miners come Saturday night.

The assayer drew his bushy graying brows together over narrowed black eyes and leaned forward until his round belly pushed up against his desk. "Did you talk to her?"

"Yeah." Lester took his time dropping into the chair opposite McGreevy. "Wouldn't mind smoking one of those cigars of yours."

"Tell me what happened with the Dawson girl," McGreevy barked. The stingy old bastard had never once offered Lester a cigar. Hadn't even asked him to take a seat in his office. Figured he was too good for the likes of Lester. But all that was gonna change. McGreevy needed him more than ever now.

"Looks like her and the old man hired themselves an Indian."

"A what?" McGreevy yanked the cigar out of his mouth and stared, bug-eyed through the cloud of smoke.

"Miz Dawson claimed he was her cousin." Lester snorted.

"But that ain't what I heard at the Golden Slipper. The man told Chester that he's a Pinkerton. Big, ugly son of a bitch. They must've hired him on for protection."

"Jesus H. Christ. A Pinkerton? You sure?"

Lester shrugged indifferently. He wasn't worried about the Indian. It didn't matter how big a man was if you took aim at his back. But he liked that McGreevy looked as if he were about to piss all over himself. "I got a powerful thirst. You got any whiskey in that desk of yours?"

"You goddam fool. Dawson wouldn't have hired a Pinkerton unless you made him suspicious."

"I done no such thing. I haven't even seen Dawson for going on three months, maybe longer."

"Why is that, Lester?" McGreevy asked, his face darkening. "I pay you to keep an eye on the man, figure out where he's getting his gold and you can't even find him. I don't know why I thought I could trust you to do a simple job."

Lester straightened, a little nervous at the way the other man's eyes shifted toward the drawer where he kept his gun. "He's been laid up at home sick. He ain't been prospecting."

"How do you know that?"

"Ask anybody in town."

"Who told them Dawson's sick? The daughter? Now she's taken up with an Indian and trading the old man's gold." McGreevy's laugh was anything but pleasant. "Not too bright, are you, boy?"

Tamping down his anger, Lester stared into the man's cold black eyes. As much as he'd like to put a bullet in the center of the fat man's forehead, he wasn't about to cross McGreevy. Not yet. Besides, he wasn't so dumb that he hadn't guessed the assayer had hired him hoping he wouldn't ask too many questions. But Lester didn't need to. Privately, he knew as well as McGreevy that Dawson's gold hadn't come from the stake he'd claimed in the hills. More likely it came from that creek that wound to the east right behind their cabin. "You got a point to make?"

McGreevy gazed thoughtfully up at the ceiling, as if Lester didn't even exist. "She might've done away with her old man herself. Ever think of that?"

"Miz Dawson?" Lester chortled. Look who was being dim. "She ain't the kind of woman who'd do a thing like that."

"When there's as much gold as I suspect there is, you'd be surprised what man, woman or child might be willing to do to get their hands on it."

"Yeah?" Lester smiled at the man's slip of the tongue.

McGreevy obviously realized he'd said too much and coughed like he'd gotten a wad of cotton stuck in his throat. He pulled out a bottle of whiskey from his bottom drawer, along with two glasses. After pouring himself a couple of jiggers, he set the bottle down on the desk and slid it toward Lester. "If the Dawsons don't want to sell the place, we need to step up our plans."

Lester poured his own measure and downed the amber liquid before saying, "What might that be?"

"Hell, use your imagination, boy."

Lester reached for the bottle again, his fingers beginning to itch at the thought of all that gold his for the taking. The nights were getting mighty cool lately. Could be that a nice big bonfire would do the trick.

MAGGIE WOKE the next morning with a start. She looked around the familiar bedroom, bathed in pink and gold from the early morning sun creeping in between the curtains, and saw nothing amiss. The door was closed, the plank floor bare where the other cot had been the night before. No call for her jumpiness, except maybe in her sleep she'd heard Cord stirring in the next room. Assuming he was still there.

She quickly grabbed her wrapper and pulled it over her white nightgown as she crept toward the door. It creaked just as it always did, but she cringed anyway, hoping she hadn't woken Cord if he were asleep. But she needn't have worried.

He lay facedown, one arm dangling to the floor, both his bare feet sticking out from the end of the quilt and hanging over the foot of the cot. He looked horribly uncomfortable and yet he seemed to sleep soundly. Maybe like her, he'd had a fitful night. Or then again, she thought sourly, maybe their encounter last night hadn't fazed him one bit.

She'd had no such luck. In fact, she was quite surprised that she'd fallen asleep at all. More than once she'd considered leaving her room and coming out here for a blunt talk with him. Each time she'd chickened out and ended up pulling the covers over her head to help forget the foolish thought.

Her gaze ran the length of his body, most if it shielded from her view by the faded quilt, and it struck her again how she'd seen more of this man than any other. Even the sight of his large bare feet produced an odd flutter in her belly. Was she being silly? Had her sisters shared the same experience when they'd first laid eyes on their husbands' bootless feet?

She shook away the rumination and immediately noticed his britches and shirt that lay in a heap near the foot of the cot. Belatedly she recalled that yesterday had been laundry day. There wasn't much she could do now. She'd insist that he buy at least a ready-made shirt in town with the money she'd gotten, but in the meantime the best she could do was air out his old clothes.

He'd been more careful about his jacket, hanging it on one of the kitchen chairs, so she ignored it and stepped lightly to gather the shirt and britches. She moved to the door with the bundle in her arms, slipped on her shoes without lacing them and pulled her wrapper more tightly against her body before going out into the brisk dawn air.

The truth be told, she was glad for something to do, something that took her outside of the four walls that had seemed to shrink with Cord's presence. She did long for a cup of hot strong coffee, especially with the draft biting into her through the thin wrap, but making coffee had to wait until he awoke.

At the clothesline, she tossed his trousers over her shoulder and then shook out his shirt before securing it to the line. The weather was perfect for the job and the shirt instantly flapped in the stiff breeze. She shook out the denim britches next, and saw something fall to the ground. After picking up the soft silky fabric, she recognized the odd style of drawers he'd been wearing yesterday.

The intimacy of handling them riled her and she quickly tossed them over the line. She was about to do the same with his trousers when she felt something in one of the pockets. She reached inside and withdrew a metal object. Black, rectangular and a bit shiny, its purpose wasn't immediately apparent. After studying the odd little contraption, she figured out that the metal was somehow folded in half. Curious, she pried it apart at the seam.

It flipped open, startling her, by buzzing and lighting up as if someone had struck a match to it. Except the lights were behind a glass casing in a rainbow of colors that made her dizzy. Below were rows of numbers. Gingerly she touched the number 5 which made a sharp sound and promptly appeared behind the glass case. Her pulse quickened. Was this some sort of Indian magic?

Fascinated, she checked his other pockets. There were keys, although much smaller and squatter than any she'd seen before. She also found a miniature square leather folder, the size of a gaming card, but finely made, with perfect, nearly invisible stitches. After glancing over her shoulder to make sure Cord hadn't come looking for her, she opened the small folder. And gasped.

A tiny likeness of Cord stared back at her. She peered closer at the portrait, distorted somewhat by a sheet of material that looked like glass covering the image. She ran her finger-nail over the hard substance. It wasn't glass but she didn't know what it was, either. There were also tiny typeset words near his likeness. She spotted Cord's full name, but it was the "State of California" that made her breath catch.

"What are you doing?"

She jumped at the angry sound of Cord's voice coming from behind her. As if she could hide her guilt, she clutched the small folder and metal box to her thudding chest, and spun toward him. Bare-chested, he had only the old quilt wrapped low around his lean hips. His legs and feet were bare, as well, and his face was as dark and terrifying as a stormy December night.

"I'm airing out your clothes," she said weakly.

"You're snooping."

"No." She swallowed around a lump of fear, backing up when he advanced threateningly. "Not on purpose."

He snatched the leather folder out of her hand, his gaze blazing when he saw the metal box, which he grabbed, too. "God, I hope you didn't turn that on. I've lost enough of the charge."

"I—I don't know what I did. But it lit up something fierce." She felt even more anxious when he scowled at her. Spotting his britches that she'd dropped on the ground, she quickly crouched to pick them up. And to avoid his harsh gaze, she flung the denim over the clothesline. "I only meant to air out your clothes," she murmured. "I swear."

She stepped back, clutching the front of her wrapper, suddenly and painfully aware of her unbound breasts beneath her gown, afraid to look at him again, afraid of this man she no longer recognized. And to think she'd been ready to… Oh, God.

Before she could stop it, a sob broke from her throat and escaped her lips.

"Ah, Maggie." His hand closed around her wrist and he drew her toward his broad chest. "I didn't mean to snap at you. There's so much to explain and not much you'll believe."

Last night she'd welcomed his touch. Not now. She wanted to run. Get as far away from him and his heathen magic as she could. "You're hurting me," she said, twisting her wrist.

He immediately released her. "I'm sorry. I didn't think I was holding that tight."

She rubbed the skin where he'd touched her, taking another cautious step back, her gaze dropping to the play of muscle across his chest as he drove a hand through his hair. He then focused on the strange objects he held in his other hand.

He sighed. "I wanted to tell you sooner, but there never seemed to be the right time."

"Tell me what."

"About where I come from."

A chilly breeze ripped through her thin cloak but she mentally shut out the cold, unwilling to be trapped inside the cabin with him. He reacted, too, goose bumps raising from his tan flesh, his brown nipples becoming hard nubs. Fisting her hands, she had to force herself to look away from his chest, disgusted with herself that even now, her traitorous body instinctively responded in that odd way she didn't yet understand.

"Look, can we go inside? It's cold out here."

She pulled her wrapper tighter and lifted her chin.

He scrubbed at his face. "This is going to sound crazy. Just keep an open mind." He held up the metal contraption and the open leather folder holding the colored likeness of him. "Have you ever seen anything like these before?"

She frowned, gave a curt shake of her head.

"That's because they haven't been invented yet."

"Wh-what are you saying?" The hair at the back of her neck stood. She immediately wished she'd taken the time to lace her boots. Loose as they were, she couldn't outrun him to the cabin. But if they moved closer to the porch...

"I'm doing this badly," he said, clearly frustrated. Or was it an act to distract her?

He needn't have bothered. His near nakedness was enough of a distraction—the way the quilt now seemed to sag lower on his hips, exposing a wedge of silky-looking black hair that arrowed down toward his privates. Even his stomach was ridged with muscle, making her reflexively squeeze her thighs together.

She forced away her attention and gulped in a breath of frigid air, while slowly moving toward the porch. Somewhere in the back of her mind it dawned on her that his drawers were hanging on the line, which meant that beneath the quilt he had to be naked. The knowledge didn't help her composure.

He moved with her. "I'm just going to come out with it, because no matter how I say it, it's going to sound crazy." He paused. "I'm from the future, Maggie. I live in the next century."

The words barely registered before she understood that the poor man was indeed crazy. She wanted to help him, she did. But fear caught in her throat, and all she could think about was getting away so that she could think straight.

She ran for the cabin, losing one shoe before she made it to the porch. She tripped on the steps, but made it inside the door. He caught her around the waist just as she was about to slam it shut. In the tussle, the quilt fell from his hips to the floor.

15

MAGGIE TRIED NOT to look down. With all her might she tried. But like a hummingbird drawn to the nectar of a flower, her gaze went straight to the shaft of male flesh she had never in her life laid eyes upon.

She put a hand to her mouth, afraid she might have said something rude or plain horrible. What that might be she couldn't begin to recall. Her breath came in short quick pants against her palm, and she couldn't look away.

Behind her, the door closed quietly, but the sound made her jump nonetheless. She moved back until her spine hit the hard wooden door. Cord braced flat palms on either side of her face, and leaned forward, his nose close to hers. "Were you planning on locking me out?"

"No." Her lying voice came out little more than a squeak.

"I thought we'd come further than that, Maggie."

He was close enough for her to touch him. She could lower her hands, move her arms so that her fingers brushed him and pretend it was an accident. That she wanted to do such a thing at all stunned her to no end.

Instead, she shoved both hands against his chest until he jerked backward and away from her. To her amazement, he'd changed. Down there. He looked bigger, harder. Smoother. Silkier. How could that be?

"Are you going to let me explain?" he asked quietly. His

voice sounded perfectly normal while every nerve ending in her body sizzled as if it had been struck by a match.

She forced her eyes level with his, saw that his gaze had been focused on her breasts but quickly rose. She clutched the wrapper tighter and noticed to her shame that her nipples had tensed into hard beads and poked at the thin muslin cloth.

Her mouth opened, but nothing came out. Probably a good thing. Yet she had to tell him this was unacceptable. That… that he couldn't stand there buck naked, staring boldly at her, and expect her to have a conversation with him.

"Ah," he said finally. "I see we have a problem." Without a hint of self-consciousness, he took another step back and gestured at his exposed privates.

She gasped, her thudding heart near to bursting. His manhood had grown bigger still. Again, it took every shred of willpower but she looked up. Only to find herself staring into his amused eyes. And after living peaceably for twenty-five years on God's earth, for the second time in twenty-fours hours, she felt very much like slapping a man across his face.

"I'd be happy to get dressed and put you out of your obvious misery," he said. "But I have no clothes."

"You do. On the clothesline." She turned to open the door but he again flattened his palm against it, keeping it shut and trapping her between solid wood and his broad body.

"True," he said, nonchalantly dislodging a curl that had tangled with her lashes. "But they're outside."

"You're free to go get them," she directed, swatting away his hand, furious at how breathless she sounded.

His mouth curved in a crooked smile. "So you can lock me out?"

"I won't." She paused, certain he'd heard the uncertainty in her voice. "How about I get them for you?"

"You'll leave."

"Not in my night clothes." She swallowed, briefly glanced down. "In the meantime, I'd thank you kindly to wrap that quilt around you."

He studied her thoughtfully for a moment. "Take this off."

"What?" She jerked her shoulder when he plucked her cloak away from her arm.

"And your shoe."

"Are you crazy?" She winced, realizing what she'd said.

"No, I'm not." He gave her a wry smile. "But I understand why you might think so and I need the chance to explain. Come on. Off." He plucked at her wrapper again. "I know you won't go far in a nightgown and no shoes."

"I will not—" She let out a shriek when he pushed the garment off her shoulders, pulling her against him, one arm encircling her, keeping her still while he freed her arms from the sleeves. She squeezed her eyes shut when she felt the hard length of him nudge her lower belly through her thin nightgown.

"I'm sorry it has to be this way, Maggie," he whispered close to her ear, his warm moist breath stirring more than her hair. "Please believe that much."

The overwhelming urge to touch him hadn't left her yet and she didn't know who she despised more, Cord or herself. "I hate you," she whispered back.

"I know." Abruptly he stepped back, and opened the door, apparently having decided to let her keep her one shoe on. "Go."

She crossed her arms over her breasts and hurried into the frigid air, minding the chill less this time. In fact it felt good on her fevered skin. How could she suffer so many mixed emotions and sensations all at once? Fear and outrage should be her only response to his ridiculous claims. Yet what she felt was so much more complicated than that. Had he used his magic to cast some sort of wicked spell on her?

Scariest of all, she didn't know who was crazier, him or her.

Thinking about the situation more carefully…she didn't fear him like she should. If she did, her body couldn't respond such as it had at the sight of his nakedness. She'd actually wanted to touch him, for heaven's sake.

A startlingly clear image of him standing in all his masculine glory sprung to mind. How he'd seemed to grow larger by the second. Never had she seen anything like it. The saints preserve her, but how she'd wanted to stare and memorize every smooth silky slope, the way he'd crowned at the end…

She nearly lost her footing as she reached the clothesline and put on her missing boot. She hadn't been wrong about his sincerity yesterday in assuring she had enough food for winter, had she? He could have taken advantage of her last night, but he hadn't. Neither of which meant he still wasn't crazy, she thought glumly.

The future, indeed. She sighed and pulled his clothes off the line and hurried back to the cabin, clutching the bundle to her breasts as a shield.

He waited at the door, and to her shameful disappointment, she saw that he'd again drawn the quilt around his waist. She handed him his clothes, and then stood shivering as she watched him sort through the heap, first pulling out his drawers.

Without hesitation, he tossed the quilt onto a kitchen chair, exposing himself, only the long shaft at the juncture of his thighs wasn't so big this time. He looked over at her with a cocked brow. "You going to watch?"

Mortified, she pressed her dry lips together and spun away, searching for her wrapper. When she couldn't find it, she grabbed the quilt he'd discarded and pulled it around her shoulders, taking care to cover her breasts. Immediately the musky masculine scent of him rose from the fabric and assaulted her senses. Without thinking, her eyes fluttered closed and she breathed in deeply.

"Mind making some coffee?"

She opened her eyes and looked over just as he fastened the snap on his britches. Averting her gaze once more, she went to the kitchen, glad for the chore of getting the coffee started. He finished getting dressed, including his shirt, and joined her in the kitchen.

"I'd offer to get more water if I didn't think you'd lock me out," he said in a weary voice.

She didn't like him standing so close. Even with the thick quilt as a barrier. "What did you do with my wrapper?"

"Come," he said, reaching for her hand. "Sit with me while the coffee is brewing. We have to talk."

She ignored his outstretched hand and buried hers in the folds of the quilt. But she did walk to the kitchen table and sink onto one of the chairs, while spying her wrapper tossed on the cot still set up near the fireplace.

With a rueful smile, he sat opposite her. And between them he placed the two strange objects she'd found, along with his gun, a few coins and some greenish paper that looked like bank notes. "Ever see any of those things before?" he asked, and she slowly shook her head. "Have a closer look. The gun is unloaded, by the way."

She tentatively picked up the leather folder that held his likeness and looked inside. "Everything is in color," she murmured aloud, not really meaning to.

"To tell you the truth, I don't know when they started taking colored photographs." He shrugged. "I'm not even sure when the camera was invented."

She eyed him skeptically. Was he fooling her? "Over fifty years ago."

"Ah. My history is rusty. What about color photos?"

"I've heard of one. Taken back east over ten years ago."

"No kidding?" He seemed genuinely surprised.

She didn't add that she hadn't actually seen any, nor had she seen such a clear likeness before. "Are these playing cards?" she asked, running her thumb over the raised numbers.

"Credit cards. You use them instead of cash. Look at the coins. You were right before, those are the actual dates they were minted. And the dollar bills."

Over the next half hour, she picked up the items one by one, studying each of them, and with growing alarm, listened to his far-fetched tale. The metal box she refused to touch, even when he flipped it open to show her the colored lights. That gadget frightened her most of all.

"You're good at trickery, I'll give you that." She folded her arms across her chest, more confused than ever. The more she thought about it, against all reason, a lot of what he'd told her made sense. He was so different from other men, in his speech, the way he dressed, even the way he smelled.

"I don't know how else to prove any of this to you." Frustration creased his face. "The women I'm looking for, they come from the future, too. The one who was a doctor, she would've known things about medicine that no one here—"

Maggie paused and put a hand to her throat. She'd heard the rumors about how the woman had brought little Billy Ray back to life, but of course she hadn't believed the whispers.

"You remember something, don't you?" He caught her hand and covered it with his.

She didn't want him touching her, not now when she was so confused and miserable. "The coffee is done." She slid her hand away from his, got up from the table, praying her shaky legs would carry her.

CORD KNEW HE WAS going to go nuts waiting around for the exchange of telegrams. But of course Maggie had been right when she pointed out that fifty miles to either town was a long way to travel and come up empty. Hard for him to imagine that fifty miles would take him the entire day. In L.A., well, that distance was like going a block. But out here, on horseback?

Once he returned home, he swore he'd never take his cell phone or his car for granted again. Or any other modern convenience he enjoyed.

He flicked the reins and the old mare lumbered forward, obviously unhappy about pulling his extra weight in the wagon. He'd tried to talk Maggie out of going into town with him. But she'd insisted, and even though he felt fairly certain he'd gotten through to her, he couldn't help but worry that as soon as they got near the sheriff's office, she'd start screaming her head off that he was some kind of lunatic.

But they made it past the livery, and the barber shop and newspaper office, and even though she'd had little to say to Cord during the trip, she nodded politely to people she knew, occasionally responding to a brief comment about the weather. Not everyone seemed cordial, and if she'd noticed the nasty stares they'd received, she hadn't let on. But Cord had observed plenty. By the time they stopped in front of the telegraph office, where two older women whispered behind their hands, while giving Maggie disdainful looks, his temper had grown hot enough to fry eggs.

Maggie greeted them by name but neither woman responded. Him, they wouldn't even spare a glance at before they turned away, their expressions pinched as if they'd suddenly smelled something bad. Maggie was too gracious to react, but her face paled and the hand she used to steady herself as she climbed down from the wagon trembled.

Out of nowhere it struck him how stupid and selfish he'd been, that he was the reason she was getting the cold shoulder. Lester had probably spread the word that Cord was staying with her at the cabin, and how unlikely it was that she had a cousin who was part Indian. Or maybe this was all about him being a half-breed, period.

Stupid ignorant fools. Hell, he'd be the fool to let the old hurt fester inside him. Their bigotry was their problem. He just didn't want it spilled over to Maggie. He tethered the old mare to the hitching rail, gritting his teeth, knowing that his unchecked anger would only cause her more trouble. "I can go in and take care of the telegrams if you need to go to the general store or check the mail," he said quietly, hoping she wouldn't run straight to the sheriff. "We can meet back here."

She lifted her chin, as if she knew why he was trying to put distance between them. "The mail won't come again for another four days. Anyway, I think it prudent that we stay together."

Their eyes met. "Maybe not," he said, second-guessing whether she understood what was happening. "You should take the wagon and I'll meet you at the edge of—"

She took his hand, kept her gaze level with his, mindless that they blocked the boardwalk. Someone walked out of the telegraph office—a man, he thought, but he didn't look, just kept his eyes on Maggie's determined face. "You need me," she said softly, ignoring the newcomer's indignant sputtering.

Cord gazed into her earnest green eyes, his senses humming, and wanted to kiss her stubborn pink lips. Screw the couple who'd stopped to openly stare. Or the coarse muttered remark about filthy Indians that he vaguely overheard. He only smiled. "Anyone ever accuse you of not being brave again, you deck 'em."

She wrinkled her cute little nose. "Deck them?"

He chuckled. "We're holding up traffic."

She frowned for a second, and then said, "Ah," slipped her arm through his, briefly glanced at a gaping older woman and said, "Afternoon, Mrs. Weaver," before, head held high, she strolled beside him into the telegraph office.

It took two hours to conclude their business, and even then they were told that they wouldn't receive a response until tomorrow. Even though the person before them had not had to wait for a reply.

Maggie had done an admirable job of ignoring the stares and whispers. At least she pretended to on the outside. Although Cord knew it couldn't be easy for her to disregard the rude manner in which she was treated by her neighbors. Anger and hurt rattled around inside of him with so much violence that by the time they were halfway home he'd felt as if he'd run a marathon.

Funny thing, he didn't give a damn about the remarks that had been aimed at him. Just a month ago he would've been spoiling for a fight with anyone who'd so much as looked at him wrong. But today, his concern had been purely for Maggie. Yet another new experience for him. This time-traveling business was really getting on his nerves.

He smiled in spite of himself. That was another thing. She believed him. As far out as the tale of him falling through time had to seem to her, she'd stayed by his side, helping him navigate the foreign waters of 1878 Deadwood. Would he have believed such a claim had their roles been reversed? Doubtful.

"What?"

He turned to look at her, sitting beside him in the front of the wagon, her hand lifted to shade her questioning eyes from the late afternoon sun, her lips slightly pursed.

"You're smiling," she said.

"I was thinking about you."

"Me?"

He pulled up on the reins until Bertha stopped in the middle of the dusty road, snorting her displeasure.

Maggie gave a short confused laugh. "What are you doing?"

"You're really something, you know that?"

Her cheeks turned that pretty pink, and she glanced over her shoulder toward town. "I may well start thinking you're crazy again."

Cord laughed, amazed that some of the tension that had built since hitting town had suddenly melted like a chunk of ice under the hot sun. "Anybody behind us?" he asked with a nudge of his head, his eyes holding hers.

"I don't think so."

"Good." He cupped his hand around the nape of her neck, and brushed her lips with his.

She didn't move, just sat frozen to the spot, letting him nibble the corner of her mouth, finally allowing him to coax her lips open with his tongue. A soft mewling sound came from deep in her throat when their tongues touched, and her body relaxed as she leaned into him.

The small act of trust and surrender filled Cord with a mixture of humility and longing that stoked an ache so deep it nearly stole the breath from his body. She tasted so damned innocent and good and sweet that his instant arousal disgusted him. He didn't deserve her pureness, her generosity of spirit, but here he was, taking everything that she was willing to give, craving more still, and he couldn't seem to stop himself.

She moved closer, and he silently condemned himself as he slid an arm around her waist to pull her tighter against him. Her inexperienced tongue lightly touched his inner cheek, ran timidly along his upper teeth and then back to his cheek. The best he could do was keep himself reined in and leave her to her exploration. The restraint nearly killed him.

He splayed his hand over her ribs, his thumb brushing the underside of her breast. She tensed slightly, her tongue withdrawing, her lips firming, but then she relaxed again, sighing into his mouth when he gently stroked her ribs.

Guilt came at him hard and fast. This was crazy. He had

no right playing with her like this. Hadn't he just put her through enough? He gentled the kiss, took a deep shuddering breath and then pressed his forehead to hers.

"I'm so sorry, baby," he whispered.

"Why?" She stiffened, pulling away, looking dazed, a little afraid, her perfect pink lips still damp from his kisses. "What did I do?"

"Not you." He shifted so that if she looked down she wouldn't be able to see how aroused he was. "You didn't do anything." He snorted. "Except be so brave."

She reared her head back, and a sad smile curved her mouth. "I'm not—"

He quickly put a finger to her lips, cutting her off, the resignation in her voice getting to him in a swift eruption of anger. "Don't say you aren't brave. I mean it, damn it." It had to have been her father who'd put that ridiculous notion in her head. Good thing the damn fool wasn't around or Cord would have to knock some sense into the guy. "I know how much being seen with me cost you today."

She waved a dismissive hand. "Those women are missing. I had to help. That's all."

He caught her hand, turned it over and planted a kiss in her palm, just as he'd once done. What the hell was he doing? Hadn't he ordered himself not to touch her again? "You didn't have to do anything, but you did, and that's what makes you brave."

"Oh, I'm not the brave one," she murmured absently, staring in fascination at her upturned palm as if it were a rare flower.

"If you say that one more time, I swear I'll—"

Her earnest eyes raised to his, her lips slightly puffy from his kisses. God, he wanted her. With a mindless urgency he'd never before experienced and couldn't grasp.

Bertha whinnied and stomped impatiently.

That, he totally understood, he thought, grudgingly releasing Maggie's hand and flicking the reins.

16

MAGGIE THOUGHT her hair would never dry as she brushed out the tangles and watched from the window as Cord carried the tub back out to the barn. In ten minutes it would have been too dark for him to have made the trip without a lantern. As it was, the soft glow of a nearly full moon was all that enabled her to see the wide breadth of his shoulders, and the long leanness of his muscled legs.

It was getting downright silly how her belly couldn't seem to stop fluttering every time she looked at him. Even while he'd taken his bath and she'd hid out in the bedroom drying her hair, she couldn't keep herself from picturing how he must've looked, wet and naked, on the other side of the closed door.

She shuddered at a flash of memory from this afternoon. Ladylike or not, she was really liking this kissing business, and she fully intended to be doing more of the same. As much as she wanted to watch him return, she was wasting precious minutes standing idly at the window so hurried back to the bedroom to use the mirror.

Her skin was a bit sunburned from the recent trips to town, and she swore she counted three more freckles than were there last week. She took a deep breath, pulled back two lengths of her hair and secured them with a short blue ribbon that matched her dress, and left the rest down. She'd just finished cleaning her teeth when she heard him stomping his boots at the front door.

Pressing a hand to her nervous belly, she checked one last time in the mirror, before leaving the room. His hair still damp, he'd gone directly to the fire, where he rubbed his hands together to ward off the chilly evening air. He looked over at her and smiled. Her heart did a funny jig.

"I wish you could see my bathroom back home, Maggie," he said, stopping to blow warm air into his cupped hands. "I have what's called a whirlpool bath. You never have to move it and there's always plenty of warm water that jets out like magic."

She nodded. "I heard there are houses back east that have rooms just for bathing. But what do you mean by jets?"

Cord frowned, and then laughed. "It's kind of hard to explain. Doesn't matter, anyway," he said and stared into the fire, his expression growing morose.

He was homesick, she assumed with a start, the notion quickly fueling a sickening dread in the pit of her stomach. And why shouldn't he be homesick? He was a stranger here, surrounded by strange customs as she'd learned today. He never intended to stay. She knew that. But when would he leave? Tomorrow? The next day?

Chilled suddenly, she moved closer to him and the fire, seeking warmth, his warmth. There was a puzzled look on his face, so she stuck out her hands, pretending to warm them.

"Want me to get you your coat and gloves?" he asked, his gaze lingering on her features.

She shook her head, wanting only for him to slip an arm around her, draw her close, but she didn't know how to ask. It didn't help that he suddenly seemed uneasy, as he pulled back his hands and shoved them deep into his trouser pockets.

"Maybe I should get some wood for later," he said, starting to move away. "Wouldn't hurt to bring in more water, either."

"Wait." She touched his arm, then promptly lowered her hand.

The haunted look of a trapped animal crossed his face. "Maggie, I, uh—"

"Is leftover ham all right for supper?" she asked quickly. She wasn't brave. She was a coward. A worthless, yellow-bellied coward who couldn't speak her mind.

"Sure." He seemed to relax, which made her want to weep. She tried to smile, but the effort seemed too great. What had she done since their ride back to make him want to withdraw from her? Dejected, she watched him walk away.

"Ah, hell." He stopped partway to the door, turned and in three long strides, roughly grabbed her forearms, and pulled her against him.

Her head fell back and, breathlessly, she stared up at his tortured face. Never had she seen him look so uncertain. "I want this," she whispered.

"You don't know what you're saying."

"I do, Cord." She moistened her lips. "I do."

He kissed the side of her mouth. "I wish I were a better man."

"No." She put a finger to his lips. "Don't."

He drew the tip into his mouth, sending a shiver down her spine, stoking a pang of longing deep inside her. She watched in fascination as he swirled his tongue around her finger before sucking it deep into his mouth. Almost as if there were a direct connection from her finger, a warm moist sensation at the juncture of her thighs made her want to squeeze her legs together.

She withdrew her hand and he let her, moving his mouth to the side of her neck, to her earlobe, as her palms settled on his shoulders. She held her breath until she couldn't possibly hold it another second, desperate to know what she should be doing in response to his eager mouth. Moving in closer so that her breasts grazed his chest, she slid her arms around him, pulling him in tighter until her nipples hardened and ached from the pressure of his strong body.

With a low groan, he swept her into his arms, and carried her into the bedroom, dimly lit from the lantern light filtering in from the kitchen. Wincing a little and flexing his scarred shoulder, he gently laid her down on the cot. She felt guilty that her weight had caused him pain, but it was quickly forgotten when he bent to unfasten the buttons down the front of her dress.

She tensed, instantly angry at herself for doing so when he hesitated and looked deep into her eyes, his a well of doubt and self-reproach. Boldly, she reached for his buttons and slid them free one by one. When his shirt finally hung open, she ran her palms over his bare chest, arching her back and closing her eyes at the exquisite feel of smooth hard muscle.

"Oh, Maggie," he whispered. "You are so beautiful."

The words rang hollow, but before she allowed the preposterousness of them to shroud her in gloom, he was impatiently tearing at her buttons, unfastening them at a speed she'd thought impossible. He parted her bodice, exposing her chemise and then startled her into opening her eyes by putting his mouth against the fabric and finding one of her hardened nipples. His tongue stroked her through the thin muslin, the moist heat of his breath dampening the cloth that clung to her heated skin, and then used his teeth to mercilessly tease her until she prayed he'd rip the chemise from her body.

She shoved at his open shirt, trying to push it off his shoulders, yet not hurt him. Then it must have sunk in what she was trying to do because Cord pulled back and shrugged out of the shirt to toss it somewhere behind him. He stared down at her breasts, lightly touched one protruding nipple through the damp fabric and gave her a crooked smile.

"What?" she asked shyly, flinging an arm across her bosom.

He moved her arm, using it to pull her to a sitting position, and then gently rolled her dress off her shoulders. After he'd helped her pull her arms free of the sleeves, he thoughtfully studied the chemise. "How does this work?"

She laughed softly. "Here," she said, lifting an arm and plucking at the ribbons that held the chemise in place.

"Ah." This new feral smile changed his face. Made her fingers still and the butterflies in her belly start fluttering around again. He moved her hand and took over the job of loosening the ribbons.

Within seconds he pulled the chemise over her head and then laid her back down on the cot, her breasts totally bared. Instinctively she crossed her arms over herself.

He bent down to kiss the back of her knuckles, the backs of her wrists, his stubbled jaw lightly scraping the tender skin over her ribs. "We can stop right now," he whispered.

She swallowed, and shook her head. "No, please."

Hesitation darkened his hazel eyes, and he kissed the tip of her nose.

Still covering herself like a frightened rabbit, she exhaled sharply, uncrossing her arms and bringing them to her sides.

He sat at the edge of the cot, splaying one large hand across her belly, but not coming close to her breasts. "I know you're nervous," he said, keeping his eyes on her face. "I am, too."

"You?" She didn't believe him, but she liked that he tried to put her at ease. Heat had long ago climbed her neck and lingered, and she knew she was as pink as a June plum but there was nothing she could do about it.

He slowly nodded. "I've never been with a virgin before."

Her cheeks burned. The desire to cover her breasts again had her fisting her hands around the soft quilt beneath her. "Why does that make you nervous?"

"Because I don't want to hurt you."

"Oh."

"But I will. A little. You know that, right?"

She hesitated, and then nodded jerkily.

The fleeting expression of dread on his face told her that her denial hadn't been quick enough. He eased away from her, and she clutched at his hand. "There's a lot I don't know," she admitted miserably. "Help me to understand. Show me."

He looked as if he'd rather be thrown from a bull, and then he gave her a gentle smile that reassured her even less. "There are things we can do that will make you feel good, but still leave you intact." He paused, cupping the weight of her right breast. "Do you get my meaning?"

She melted into his touch, briefly closing her eyes and nodding mindlessly. Truth be told, she wasn't at all sure what he was talking about, and didn't care. She wanted him to keep touching her. And kissing her. And making her skin tingle and heat at the same time.

He tugged at her skirt, and she braced herself when she knew he meant to pull her dress off. A few buttons near her waist remained fastened and he had to free them before drawing the voluminous skirt down her hips. She lifted her bottom off the cot, until she was left in only her thin pantalets, shivering under the heat of his gaze.

"You, too," she said, her breath catching.

"Tell me."

"Take off your trousers." The knowledge that the daring words had actually made it past her lips filled her with a heady sense of power she'd never known before.

He didn't hesitate, but unsnapped the denim. She caught a peek of the silky drawers beneath his britches before he shoved them both down his hips and then kicked the heap against the wall. She tried not to stare, she did, but her gaze riveted to the long hard length of him. Unprepared for the primal response that stirred deep in her belly, she'd lain there while he loosened the drawstring waist of her pantalets and then tossed them aside before she even knew what he'd done.

She bent her knees slightly, fighting the shyness that washed over her, yet not wanting to discourage him. He sat on one side of the cot, looking at her as if he'd never seen a naked woman before, and stroked a hand down the side of her thigh. She automatically curled her body toward him, and his hand slid around to mold the fleshy curve of her buttocks. She arched her back, and he lowered his head to dust a kiss across first one breast, and then the other.

She started to relax under his feathery touch when he closed his lips on her nipple, tugging, suckling, his warm moist breath both terrifying and exciting her at the same time. Heedlessly she reached for him, not knowing what she sought, her fingers digging into the hard muscles of his thighs. By accident she felt his maleness, against the backs of her fingers, silky smooth yet rock hard, around it a nest of soft, springy hair.

Maggie froze. Dare she turn her hand over, let his shaft rest against her palm? She wanted to, yet she wasn't sure she had the courage.

Cord lifted his head. "Do you want to touch me, Maggie?" he asked hoarsely.

She swallowed, and nodded, but couldn't seem to make her hand move.

He trailed his fingertips over her knuckles, his touch a light dusting. "Have you ever seen a man naked before?"

She widened her eyes at the outlandish notion and briefly met his gaze, before hers flickered away. "No."

He picked up her hand and turned it over, palm up. To her amazement, his wasn't too steady. It made it easier to look at him, see the unexpected vulnerability in his face. See the slight tremble of his shoulders. He was actually trembling.

Why? Her gaze went to the scar that curved around the top of his shoulder, and then she met his eyes.

Without looking away from her, he lifted her hand to his lips and kissed her palm, and then he wrapped her fingers around his smooth hot manhood. She jumped at the initial touch, as if he'd scorched her, and then watched in awe as the trembling in his shoulders spread through his chest. His jaw clenched so tight the veins stood out along the side of his neck.

Slowly she squeezed her hand around him. Her heart and stomach lurched at the same time. Cord groaned softly, his eyes drifting closed as he moved against her hand. Her courage faltered and she released him.

He opened his eyes, and his mouth curved in a slight smile. "That felt good, Maggie," he said, pushing a hand into her hair and burying his fingers there. "Really good."

"I didn't hurt you."

His smile widened. "Not even a little." His attention went to her breast and with his other hand he pinched her nipple between his thumb and forefinger, before lowering his head and rolling his tongue over the sensitive spot.

The pleasure of his touch made her squirm, made her grow damper still between her thighs. He shifted his weight then, abandoning her nipple, and she couldn't figure out what he meant to do when he tried to stretch out but ended up growling in frustration.

Abruptly he straightened, groaned as he got to his feet. "I'll be right back."

She watched with wide-eyed shock as he left the bedroom, and then her entire body heated with shame when her gaze fell onto her wanton nakedness. She tried desperately to pull the quilt over herself but her weight trapped the cover beneath her rump. Just as she rolled to her side, Cord appeared in the doorway carrying the other cot.

"Hey." He set the cot down and then casually bent to kiss her on the mouth as if he'd done it a hundred times, and then to her utter astonishment, he dropped a kiss on her quivering belly.

Using the distraction, he pried the quilt from her fingers. He straightened and stood back, brazenly looking at her, from the point of her chin down to her toes, which she could barely keep from curling.

Without the cot blocking her view, she got a good look at him, too. But the light came from the open door behind him, and she couldn't see as much as she would've liked. As if reading her mind, he pushed the spare cot up against hers and said, "I'm going to get the lantern."

"You're bringing it in here?" The idea suddenly didn't appeal. He'd see every freckle, every callus on her elbows and hands. Heavens, he'd see her private woman's place. She gasped at the thought and squeezed her thighs together. "You can't do that."

He crouched down to toy with one of her nipples, his face in shadow, but she knew he was smiling. "Why not?"

"Because."

"Ah." The smile reached his voice. "I see."

"Don't make fun of me," she managed in a pathetic whisper because when he touched her like this it was hard to think and talk at the same time.

"Oh, there's a lot of things I want to do to you, Maggie Dawson. Making fun of you doesn't even come close." It was the low rumbling timbre in his voice more than his words that stole her breath away.

She said not a word as he disappeared again, but he was only gone a few seconds before he brought in the lantern. She shut her eyes against the light, not because it was too bright but because in the flame her courage seemed to flicker. She wanted him, more than she would've guessed possible a week ago. There was no doubt or regret swirling around inside of her. Only a yearning she couldn't name, a primitive desire that burned even hotter than his touch.

A noise stirred her and she opened her eyes to see him setting the lantern on the floor in the corner, sending the fire's soft glow up like a canopy over the room. His backside muscles flexed, and her palms itched to follow the contours that formed the shallow dimple in each sculpted cheek. With a thrill she realized that she could touch him there if she wanted, run her hands along the tautness of his skin, feel every curve and ridge of sinew. He wouldn't deny her.

He made sure the cots butted up against each other, and then stretched out alongside her. "You look pretty smug." One side of his mouth lifted as he brushed a lock of hair away from her eyes. "What are you thinking?"

A strangled laugh escaped her lips. "Nothing."

"Right." His hand went back to her breast as if there had been no interruption, as if touching her were the most natural thing in the world. "I'll get it out of you," he said with a devilish smirk as he lowered his mouth to her nipple. "One way or another."

With his lips pressed to her breasts, his last words came out garbled, and it made her laugh unexpectedly. She felt his smile against her skin, and with an odd mixture of pleasure and wistfulness, she wondered if this comfortable union of humor and intimacy was how it was with married people. Yet she couldn't imagine Mary or Clara and their husbands behaving so… Well, maybe Clara.

No, not even the sweetly irrepressible Clara had this kind of bond with William. The notion made Maggie's blood sing through her veins, and she cautiously curled toward him so that her lips met the scar at his shoulder. She lightly kissed the marred area, wanting to soothe, wanting things she couldn't begin to name.

He lifted his head and looked at her with glazed eyes, before gathering her close and kissing her so hard on the mouth that her head tipped back. His heart hammered against her breastbone, oddly reassuring her that she was safe, that she was exactly where she was supposed to be. For no matter how fervent his mouth, his strong arms held her tenderly when he could so easily have crushed her.

Cord moved over her, using his knee to force her thighs apart. For a moment, she fought panic, instinctively wanting to scramble out from beneath him. The feeling quickly passed, and she relaxed under his expert mouth, under the ministration of his gentle hand as he used his thumb to dry the moisture that seeped to the outside corner of her eye.

His other hand he slid between her thighs, and her composure again slipped at the bold intimacy of his touch. She jerked beneath him, and though he stilled his hand, he didn't retreat.

"Shh," he murmured, and it was only then that she knew she'd cried out. "It's okay, baby."

"Wh-what are you doing?" she asked in a small voice, her thighs clamped around his hand.

"I'm going to touch you. But I won't hurt you."

Her breath came in quick small pants. She was embarrassingly wet there, and he would feel it and wonder, and she didn't know what to do or say.

"Trust me," he whispered.

She didn't even think about it, because amazingly, deep down, she did, and slowly opened up for him.

17

MAGGIE SHIVERED when he skimmed his hand along the inside of her thigh. She tried to be calm but still struggled against the occasional urge to push him away. His fingers brushed the nest of curls that guarded her deepest feminine secret, and her entire body snapped taut.

"Ah, you're so wet for me," he said quietly, burying his face between her breasts.

She whimpered in humiliation and covered her face with her hands.

He lifted his head and smiled, using his teeth and chin to force her hands away from her face. "No, that's good, Maggie. It's a good thing." His honeyed words distracted her while he forged deeper, the tips of his fingers dipping into the crevice of her womanhood.

She thought she would die. Right there. As naked as the day she was born. And no one would find her until the spring thaw, but that was all right because…

He slid a finger all the way inside her, and she came up off the cot, at least her shoulders did, because he was kissing her belly, teasing her nipples with his other hand, holding her down. She arched her back, and let her shoulders ease back onto the cot, confused at the sudden tension building slowly, relentlessly, inside of her.

His mouth moved up to her breast, to her chin and then he

planted light kisses on either side of her mouth. "You okay?" he asked in a soft voice.

"I think so," she said, whimpering when he used his thumb in a small circular motion that started a whole new kind of pressure.

Heat surged through her until her skin prickled from the liquid fire coursing along her nerve endings. She clutched Cord's muscled arm, not because she wanted him to stop, but because the growing sense that she was losing control was both exciting and frightening and she needed his support, needed to know that he wouldn't leave her.

"That's it," he whispered, his moist breath bathing her ear. "Stay with me."

A strange noise came from deep down in her throat as a rush of warmth flooded her belly. Her nails dug deep into the flesh of his arm. She had to be hurting him, but he didn't move away, just stroked her hair and dusted kisses over her face, down the side of her neck. When the pressure seemed too great, she bucked against his hand, dug deeper still into his flesh, and cried out when the earth-shattering spasms started.

CORD CRADLED HER to his chest as her orgasm subsided and the thrashing and convulsive jerking had stopped. As aroused as he'd been, he surprisingly started to calm now. She turned to bury her face against his chest and clung to him. He kissed her hair, held her tight.

"It wasn't so bad, was it?" he asked, suppressing a smile and stroking her arm, her pale satiny skin nearly gleaming in the soft glow of the lantern.

She didn't move for a long time, and when she finally looked at him, her face tearstained, he instantly sobered. "It was…" She hiccupped. "It was wonderful."

He exhaled slowly and used his thumb to brush the hair

away from her damp flushed cheeks. Her brows puckered in a frown, and guessing at her sudden concern, he said, "Technically, you're still a virgin. No man will know otherwise."

"You mean, we're done? We're stopping?"

At the earnestness in her widened eyes, he chuckled. He couldn't help it. "There are other things we can do," he said slowly.

"Show me." She put a shy hand on his belly.

His body immediately reacted, roared out of hibernation with a sharp twitch of his cock. He bit back a curse. "We have to be careful," he warned. "You understand?"

"I know you're trying to be honorable."

He kissed the tip of her nose, and when her lashes lowered, he kissed each eyelid. She didn't understand how difficult this was for him. He was barely holding it together as it was. His gaze roamed the scattering of freckles across her nose and cheeks down to the pebbled tips of her small perfect breasts.

The hell of it was that the desire burning inside him went beyond wanting physical release. She aroused feelings in him he refused to label, feared dwelling upon.

"What if I want more?" Her hand moved dangerously close to the head of his eager cock.

He briefly closed his eyes and tightened his arms around her. "Then you tell me what you want," he said more harshly than he intended, and when she shrunk away from him, he sighed with regret. "I'm trying to do the right thing here."

Her lips curved in a watery smile. "I know, and I—" Her chin went up. "I release you from taking the high ground."

He chuckled, shook his head. "Heaven help me."

She turned her entire body brazenly toward him and stared at his glistening penis with fascination. "You're wet, too," she said and stuck out her forefinger, but was hesitant to make contact.

"Touch me," he whispered brokenly.

She carefully touched her finger to him. Through clenched teeth, he sucked in a breath. Her probing gaze went to his face and then back down, and with new confidence she pressed her palm bluntly against the slick crown.

"That's enough," he said, his voice raspy as he strained away from her hand.

"No." She inched closer. "Please, Cord."

"Maggie, you don't understand." Sweat had popped out at the back of his neck. His cock throbbed with urgency.

"Please," she said again, pleadingly, shyly, and she parted her thighs slightly.

"I'll hurt you." He'd already shifted his weight, his body anxious to be buried deep inside her even while mentally ordering himself to ignore her invitation. She was caught up in the moment and didn't understand that what they did could brand her for life.

"You won't." She lay back, readying herself, a serene smile lifting the corners of her pink lips. "I trust you."

"Maggie…"

"I'm a grown woman, Cord," she whispered, and wrapped her fingers around his shaft, pumping once, twice, her awkward bashfulness more seductive than the most practiced Hollywood temptress.

He forced her legs farther apart and positioned himself over her. Grasping her hips, he drew her toward him. Slowly, his entire body quivering with restraint, he pressed himself into her, but the entry was so tight that it gave him a moment's pause. She tensed, too, but she was wet and ready and with a small lift of her hips urged him on.

Knowing there wasn't any way he could spare her pain the first time, he pushed into her, felt the resistance, saw the fear flicker in her eyes and then steeled himself as he drove into her with one hard thrust. She cried out, the plaintive sound slashing through him like a knife, and he stilled.

"Shh, baby, it's okay. That's the worst of it." Then he moved slowly, letting her get used to the feel of him. The tone of her moaning changed, and she was wet again, the rigidity of her body melting as she lifted her hips for him. The strain of holding back nearly killed him, and he moved deeper and deeper inside her, gaining momentum until she cried out again.

He came then, violently, his body a quivering mass of unfamiliar emotion with his final release. Completely spent, he sank down on top of her, barely capable of keeping his weight from crushing her. She lifted her face and sweetly kissed his chin, and then sighed with contentment.

God, he hoped she didn't hate him later.

AFTER A DISMALLY overcast morning, the threat of sleet thick in the air, sunlight wedged its way between two undecided clouds. Cord hauled up a bucket of water from the well, and watched Maggie gingerly pick her way toward the barn. She was still sore from their lovemaking, and yet had refused to let him tackle the morning chores alone. Probably because it had been almost noon before they'd actually rolled out of bed, and she'd been worried sick about relieving the poor cow of its milk.

But with the two of them working together it hadn't taken long to water and feed the horses, fork down fresh hay from the loft, scatter feed for the chickens and replenish the wood supply in the cabin. Cord flexed his stiff shoulder. Later, after he went to the telegraph office, he'd split some wood. The outside pile was getting too low, and if her sister didn't show up soon, Maggie wouldn't have enough heat for the winter.

There he went again, thinking about what would happen after he left. He yanked the bucket too hard and water splashed the front of his jeans. It was hopeless. He couldn't turn off the anxious thoughts that had started the second the fog of sleep had lifted from his brain. He was acting like a friggin' mother hen. What was that about? Maggie had done fine without him. She'd be fine after he left.

He'd surprise her, he decided, and bring in the tub. While he split wood, she could soak in warm water. He tested the mobility of his sore arm, wincing at the protest of muscles and tendons. Hauling in enough water was going to be a pain in the ass after the way he'd abused his arm last night, but she deserved the pampering.

He met up with her as she left the barn carrying a basket of eggs. The slow measured way she maneuvered the rocky path made him smile sympathetically. "I hope you're planning on taking it easy the rest of the day." He slid an arm around her waist and planted a swift kiss on her unsuspecting mouth.

She bumped him with her shoulder, a grin lifting her lips. "Such liberties you take, sir, in broad daylight no less."

He cupped the weight of her breast. "After I get back from town, I'll show you the meaning of taking liberties."

"You're terrible," she crowed, but her eyes gleamed with anticipation, the basket of eggs forgotten, as she lifted her chin and pressed her mouth to his, readily parting her lips, eagerly meeting his tongue with hers.

It took them a moment to hear the pounding of hooves and, startled, they broke apart. Guilt washed over Maggie's face as she tensely awaited the arrival of the two riders who were close enough to have seen their intimate embrace.

Cord's gut clenched when he recognized the deputy was approaching. If he said one derogatory word to Maggie about what he'd seen, Cord would tear him apart with his bare hands.

Without waiting for Maggie to greet the men as they neared, he brusquely asked, "What can we do for you, Deputy?"

The scorn on Lester's face left no doubt as to what he'd seen. He focused on Maggie. "I see your *cousin* is still here."

Maggie blanched slightly at the man's sneering emphasis, and when Cord made a sudden move toward the deputy, she touched his arm, smiled bravely and said, "Why, Deputy, I'm flattered that you've taken such a keen interest in me."

Lester's face darkened ominously and he turned to spit onto the dusty ground. Even the wiry bearded man sitting on the roan beside the deputy cast him a nervous glance. "Your pa around?"

"No."

Still refusing to acknowledge Cord, Lester said, "Word around town is that you hired yourself a Pinkerton."

Maggie issued a short unconcerned laugh. "Really?"

Cord forgot about how pissed off he was, how a minute ago he'd wanted to rearrange the deputy's face. Bowled over by Maggie's spunk, Cord stared at her with pride and admiration.

"Me, I don't believe it," Lester said with an evil twist of his mouth. "Who ever heard of the Pinkerton Agency using a filthy Indian?"

"You despicable little—" Maggie's hands curled into fists and she lurched toward the deputy.

Taken by surprise at her vehemence, Cord caught her around the waist. "He's not worth it," he whispered. "He's nothing."

Lester laughed crudely. "Letting a woman fight your battles for you?"

Cord coolly met the man's cold black eyes, and calmly said, "Climb down and ask me again."

The bearded man pulled on his reins and wheeled his horse around. "Come on, Lester," he said in a tobacco-rough voice.

The deputy held Cord's gaze a moment longer, and then he smiled. "Almost forgot." Holding up a piece of paper, he dropped it to the ground. He let his horse prance over the sheet a few times before reining in the animal and galloping after the other man.

Cord saw that it was the telegram he'd been waiting for even before he picked up the piece of paper. But his thoughts were on Maggie. How fiercely she'd stuck up for him. Emotion clogged his throat when it struck him that Masi had been the only other person to give that much of a damn about him.

MAGGIE POURED them each a cup of coffee and then joined Cord at the kitchen table. Guilt gnawed at her as she watched him painstakingly use his palms to press out the creases from the trampled paper. She knew the only reason he was here was to find the missing women and that telegram could be an important clue. But she also knew it might be what took him away from her. Heaven help her, but she wasn't ready to say goodbye.

"At least Lester saved us a trip to town," she said, hoping her voice sounded normal.

"What?" Cord answered distractedly, peering intently at the smeared writing. Then he shook his head, a long lock of his black hair falling across his forehead.

She automatically reached over and brushed it away from his face, and then quickly withdrew, suddenly shy that she'd done something so familiar. He looked up, his smile extending to his hazel eyes. Her heart thudded. After last night it was ridiculous that such a simple gesture should fluster her.

"I think we might have something here," he said, and went back to studying the telegram. "Looks like Hay Camp currently has a woman doctor. I'm assuming that's unusual."

Maggie nearly spit out the sip of coffee she'd just taken and quickly covered her mouth, nodding.

He frowned thoughtfully. "That's what I thought. Wish they would've given her name. Might have. Hard to tell." He squinted at the tattered paper. "Damn that Lester."

"Would the telegraph office have a copy?" She'd never used the service before so she didn't know.

He shrugged. "I have no idea. In my time, we use e-mails, wire transfers, cell phones…"

Slowly their eyes met, and she quickly averted hers and hid behind her cup, unwilling to let him see the pain she struggled with. "I'm sure you're anxious to get back."

"Maggie." He set aside the telegram and reached for her hands, tugging persistently when she stubbornly gripped the chipped china cup. "I still have to go into town."

That's not what she'd expected him to say, and startled, she relented and let him take one of her hands and press it between his two larger ones. "Why?"

"Come here." His voice lowered, his eyes gleaming with mischief.

"What?" She smiled in spite of herself.

"Come here, and I'll show you."

He kept hold of her hand, while she rose and rounded the table. He swung his legs out from beneath it, planted his boots a foot apart and pulled her onto his lap. He didn't give her a second to anticipate what came next, but forcefully covered her mouth with his, so hard she couldn't breathe.

She finally had to pull back for air, and he moved his mouth to her throat, trailed the tip of his tongue to her ear and lightly bit her lobe. When his mouth came back to hers, she tasted his desperation, and knew this was the beginning of the end for them.

It took all of her willpower but she drew back and regarded him seriously. "You're leaving, aren't you?"

Regret shadowed his face. "You knew I would."

"I mean, now." She swallowed, afraid she'd cry, but she couldn't. Not in front of Cord. It wouldn't be fair. "You're leaving today."

"No, Maggie." He touched her cheek. "Not today."

She sagged against him, and then a thought occurred to her and she straightened. "You're going to town to send another telegram to see if it's her." They'd have to wait for the reply. That gave her another day with him.

He shook his head. "I don't want to spook her into running. It's best if I show up unannounced."

"Why are you— You can't go after Lester. I wouldn't care if you beat the man senseless, but he has friends, you'd be out-numbered." Her voice broke. "Please don't."

He grinned and stroked her arm. "I wouldn't mind beating him senseless, too, but I have other business."

She studied his face, considered his reluctance to explain, and finally understood. "You don't need to sell your watch."

His expression hardened. "This isn't up for discussion—"

"I have something to show you." She slid off his lap and disappeared into the bedroom. She dug through her dresser for the few nuggets she kept handy, and then took them to Cord.

He stared down at the palm of her outstretched hand, and then into her eyes. "Damn, that's a lot of gold."

She smiled serenely. "There's much more where that came from."

18

HE'D DREAMT AGAIN. Cord opened his eyes and blinked at the darkness, the fog of sleep still heavy at the edges of his consciousness. No moonlight filtered in from the window. The curtains had been drawn tightly to help keep out the chill air. Curled up beside him, Maggie slept soundly.

He lightly kissed her hair, though not wanting to wake her. How he wished she and Masi could have met. The sudden thought startled him, and as the fragments of his dream filtered through his brain, he acknowledged Masi had been present. She had spoken to him, pointing. There had been an eagle, flying toward an oversized moon. Before he could make sense of it though, the vision evaporated.

The moon. His grandmother had said something about the moon being full. Something important. But what? Sweat bathed his skin. He had to remember. Panic mounted inside him, which was stupid. He'd never believed in Masi's dream prophecies. But it didn't matter how he tried to reason with himself, his mind struggled with an overwhelming need to remember.

Carefully, he shifted away from Maggie and swung his feet to the floor. His mouth was dry, his skin clammy. He needed a drink of cool water. His eyes adjusted to the darkness and he made his way to the bedroom door. Fire still smoldered in the fireplace, the dim glow illuminating the way to the kitchen.

The pitcher Maggie kept with water was full, and he poured some into the cup he'd used for his coffee.

As he sipped, his gaze wandered to the window where the curtain parted. He caught a partial glimpse of the moon, and another memory washed over him. Nothing vivid, more a sense that the dream had been a warning.

Go north and the next full moon will take you home. Masi's voice rang in his ears as if she stood in the room right beside him. He looked around, half-expecting to see her brown smiling face. But he was alone. Just as he'd been for the past eighteen years. That is, until Maggie.

IT WAS NINE, the sun had risen only two hours ago, but the sky was so dark with threatening clouds that it might have been closer to sundown. Cord swung the ax one final punishing time, splitting the last of the logs in two, his shoulder aching so badly that he thought his arm would fall off. Damn stupid thing to do knowing he had to ride the fifty miles to Hay Camp on horseback. But the woodpile was low and he'd ended up spending yesterday afternoon making love to Maggie instead of restocking it.

He hoped her sister came soon. At this point he thought about convincing Maggie to risk telegramming Mary. If necessary, Maggie could get a room at one of the hotels in town while she waited. Hell, she had enough gold to pay her way. He still couldn't believe the stash she and her father had been sitting on, and panned right from the creek not far from their cabin. At least that was one worry off his shoulders. Not only would she not starve, but Maggie was actually a very rich woman.

He was going to miss her. The mere thought that after tomorrow he'd probably never see her again brought a stab of pain so violent he reeled back a step.

"How long have you been out here?" She stood in front of him, shivering, tightly clutching her thin wrap around her shoulders, staring at the mound of wood. "You've been up for a while."

"Yeah." He used the back of his sleeve to wipe his forehead, taking in the long tangle of auburn curls that cascaded over her shoulders and trailed down her breasts. He sheathed the ax blade, and then went to her, pulling her into his arms and kissing her surprised mouth.

She broke away first. "What's wrong?"

"I kiss you good morning and you ask me what's wrong?"

She didn't smile at his teasing, only looked at him with sad, inquiring eyes that tore a hole in his gut.

"It's cold." He slid an arm around her shoulders, and they headed toward the cabin.

She leaned into him, a tremor passing through her body. He chose to believe it was from the cold. "Looks like snow."

He stopped at the porch and stared up at the dark overcast sky. The last thing he needed was inclement weather for his trip north. "Kind of early."

"Not really."

He sighed, and pushed open the front door. The fire he'd started earlier had been reduced to an orange glow. He went to throw on another log. She headed for the coffeepot.

"Look, Maggie—"

"I know—" They both spoke at the same time.

"Go ahead," Cord said, and she shook her head. "No, you."

He drew a hand over his face, covering his mouth for a moment. "Let's sit down."

Pressing a hand to her belly, she nodded jerkily and joined him at the table. Her eyes remained carefully noncommittal as they met his.

"I want you to move into town," he explained, and her lashes lowered. "You'll be safer there. Especially if your sister doesn't show up. You have money, Maggie, there's nothing stopping you from getting on that stage by yourself if you—"

"It's all right, Cord. You needn't worry about me." She bravely lifted her chin. "You should leave before it snows."

He stared at her, thinking about his dream, dread gripping his insides like a vise. His fear wasn't simply about telling her that he might not be back, it went far deeper. So deep that he didn't understand the conflicting emotions swirling inside him. Of course he wanted to find the Winslow sisters, and return to his life in L.A. Simple. That should be his only goal. But it also meant never seeing Maggie again.

When had this shift in him happened? Why was this so damn hard? Hell, it was more likely that the dream meant nothing. Yeah, he might find the Winslow sisters up north, and they would know no more than he did about how to return to L.A. By tomorrow night he could be back here, asking Maggie to put him up again. All that full moon business meant was that people got a little crazier. Apparently, him included.

Still, the feeling nagged at him. Enough that he had to warn her. It would be unfair not to. He steeled himself for her reaction. "You know I may not be back."

She blinked. "Yes," she whispered brokenly.

"Ah, Maggie." He roughly covered her tightly clasped hands. "It's not for sure, but I may not have a choice. Do you understand?"

She moistened her lips. "I could go with you to Hay Camp," she said, a trace of desperation in her voice. "You might need my help. After you…if you don't— Later, I can get back here by myself."

He got up, pulled her to her feet and rested his forehead against hers. "This is hard for me, too."

She sagged against him, and he cupped her bottom, gathering her close, inhaling the warm sweet scent of her. The

thought of leaving her tore him up inside. A humiliating lump
lodged in his throat. Hell, he'd known her barely a week, and
he was far from a let's-play-house kind of guy. So how did
feeling as if his guts were being torn out make any sense?

He took a deep breath, trying to ignore how empty he felt.
He needed a clear head, he needed to think. But only one
thought seemed to form with any clarity. What if she did go
with him? Not to Hay Camp, but to L.A. Could it work, he
wondered, his heart beginning to race. Whatever catalyst had
transported him here should work for her? Maybe the Winslow sisters would know the answer. Maybe his reason for
being here wasn't just to find the two women. Maybe Masi
had sent him to find Maggie.

"Listen, Maggie." He pulled back to look at her, his heart
hammering his chest. Her eyes were wide, her pupils dilated,
her gaze fixed on him. A faint rosy blush stole across her
cheeks, the corners of her mouth lifting as she waited expec-
tantly. She was still an innocent in so many ways.

She'd hate L.A. And the people. Hell, even the crowd he
hung out with were mostly sharks. The materialism and
vanity and blind ambition that had been as much a fabric of
his life as breathing would make her miserable. How could
he do that to her?

So why had he allowed himself to fall into such a state?
Didn't he deserve better? He shook his head, breathed in
deeply. Lack of sleep was making his thinking fuzzy. Of
course he wanted his old life back. All he had to do was keep
his eye on the prize. Returning with the Winslow sisters would
change everything for him. The publicity would be enormous.
His phone would start ringing again. The tabloid offers alone
would be enough to line his pockets for life. He'd be on top
of the world again. Have anything he ever wanted.

"Cord?"

He snapped out of his trance, and stared into Maggie's guileless green eyes. Her cute freckled nose was wrinkled slightly and she looked barely twenty. The vultures back home would eat her alive. "Nothing, baby," he said, and kissed the tip of her nose. "Nothing."

THE WAY HE KISSED HER was different. So was the way he'd carefully removed her shoes and stockings, took his time unfastening each button of her shirtwaist, and then slowly stripping off her dress. As he loosened the ribbons from her chemise, he tenderly kissed each patch of skin he exposed before going to the next bow. When he'd finally tossed the muslin aside, he nuzzled first one breast, and then the other, with such aching gentleness that Maggie wanted to weep. When he removed her bloomers, again he ministered to her with agonizing slowness that left her trembling and even closer to tears.

But she wouldn't cry, she told herself. Not in front of him. Even though each unhurried act screamed that this might be the last time he touched her. But maybe she was overreacting. After all, it was already midafternoon. Too late to ride so far today. Which meant they still had tonight.

The thought of spending their last night together bathed her in gloom and threatened her resolve to remain dignified. She had so many questions she wanted to ask him, but fear stopped her every time. He'd said he may not have a choice about coming back. She'd told him she understood, but did she really? Would he suddenly disappear into thin air? Would he have warning before being sent back to the future? Did he know more than he was willing to share with her? The whole thing seemed so mysterious and pagan that she wasn't sure she wanted to know more. She only knew that she didn't want him to go. And that she had no say in the matter.

Cord molded his hand to the curve of her hip, and lightly nipped her lower lip. He pulled back to look at her, his mouth curved in a smile that quickly faded. "What's this?" Using the pad of his thumb, he wiped a tear that had seeped from her eye.

Mortified, she quickly blinked away any other unchecked tears. "Kiss me."

"Maggie." He brushed his fingers across her cheek.

With a single-mindedness she didn't know she possessed, she freed his shirt buttons and struggled to push the shirt off his shoulders.

He winced when the heel of her palm smacked the scarred area. Quickly he captured her hand and kissed the back of it. His expression seemed strained, and she knew she'd hurt him.

"I'm sorry," she said.

"It's okay, but let's slow down."

"You shouldn't have chopped all that wood." She heard the accusation in her voice but didn't understand it. "How can you ride to Hay Camp? You should wait for the stage. Maybe in a couple of days—" Desperation had sunk its prickly claws into her so deep she almost missed the pity in his eyes. Silencing herself, she summoned all the courage she could muster, took his face between her hands and kissed him as if it was the last time.

CAREFUL NOT TO wake her, Cord quietly carried his clothes out of the bedroom and then dressed quickly in front of the fire, his gaze going to the window. He didn't have much time.

The sun was already low on the horizon, probably an hour or two away from setting. He should've left hours ago, as soon as Maggie had fallen asleep, but he'd dozed off himself. Damn it, the last thing he wanted to do was travel at night. But now he had no choice. Not if he believed any of Masi's dream visit.

He strapped on his shoulder holster and gun, slipped on his

blazer and checked his pockets to make sure he had his phone and wallet and the small pouch of gold dust Maggie had given him "just in case." He hadn't wanted to accept it, but she'd stubbornly insisted and in the end it wasn't worth wasting the time arguing with her. Especially since the woman was filthy rich. He was genuinely thankful for that.

A cloud eclipsed the sun, and darkness fell over the cabin, sending a shiver of foreboding down his spine. With no time to linger, he went to the bedroom door, hesitating when a floor plank creaked beneath his weight. Maggie lay on her back, her long curly hair spread out around her face, her pink lips slightly parted. She looked so beautiful and peaceful, and it took everything he had in him not to go to her and kiss her one last time. Fearing he'd wake her, he stayed in the doorway and watched her sleep, the pain in his chest growing unbearably.

Eventually he turned away, grabbing the hat that had belonged to her father and that she'd given Cord. He focused on saddling the chestnut they'd agreed he'd take, and tried not to dwell on the fact that a minute ago might be the last time he ever saw Maggie again. He gave the saddle a final cinch and climbed on.

He'd been here nearly a week, had found his cell phone and money useless, had to opt for an outhouse and haul water into the cabin, and still he couldn't get it through his head that it wasn't possible to simply pick up a phone and call her from Hay Camp. That if and when he returned to L.A. there was no means of contacting her. He'd never know what became of her, if her sister showed up or if she made it to San Francisco. The thought was too painful to consider and he pushed it aside.

He rode as far as the ponderosa pine that stood where the path to the cabin turned into the road to town, and reined in and wheeled the chestnut around. Why he punished himself with a lingering look at the cabin he didn't know. His chest still throbbed with an ache he'd never before experienced. But if he thought staring at the lonely cabin tucked away in the tall grass at the bend in the creek would give him any relief he was sadly mistaken.

Even the snorting chestnut seemed reluctant to leave, and with ruthless determination, Cord dug in his heels and raced toward Deadwood. The air had grown increasingly chilly, the threat of snow becoming more real, and he turned up his collar, ignored the discomfort in his shoulder and prayed for another hour of daylight. Within minutes he saw that he was close to town and wished he knew a way to avoid Main Street but he couldn't risk getting lost. Time was slipping away.

A saloon brawl that had spilled onto the street near the badlands slowed him down, yet he managed to make it to the other end of town in good stead. But here the road seemed to disappear into a web of smaller camps. Tents had been set up as temporary shelters, interspersed with shacks, so shoddy they appeared less reliable than their canvas neighbors.

Cord paused, decided on the fork in the road that looked more well-traveled, and then headed past a throng of Chinese workers hanging laundry on clotheslines. The road took him north through a shallow creek and past some scrub brush for about a quarter of a mile, and then seemed to circle back toward the other end of town. He stopped, cursing under his breath, afraid he'd wasted precious time. And then he heard voices coming from a thicket of trees. Odd because he wasn't that close to town.

Instinctively he tried to move silently, using the dense pines for cover, as he urged Red in the direction of what sounded like a heated argument. As he got closer he thought he recognized the deputy's voice. The hair on the back of Cord's neck rose. He ducked his head and moved in as close as he dared, not close enough that he could actually hear what they said.

But it was Lester, all right, along with three other men, two of them holding rifles and unlit torches. The third man, the one Lester argued with, was fashioning two more torches out of strips of rags. They wore bandanas around their necks, loose like, ready to pull up over the lower parts of their faces. Obviously they were up to no good. Hell, the torches alone were a red flag. People used lanterns, and besides it wouldn't be dark for another hour.

Not his problem, Cord reminded himself, and quietly backed up. He had only a matter of hours to reach Hay Camp and find the Winslow sisters while the moon was full. Let the sheriff worry about Lester and his friends. Whatever they were up to.

Ten minutes later, he stopped at a creek to water the chestnut. Between Cord's mind drifting back to Maggie and anticipating what he'd find in Hay Camp, he'd been riding the gelding too hard. He waited impatiently, shifting from one foot to the other, as Red lapped the cold water, the scene with Lester replaying itself in Cord's head. The guy was supposed to be a goddam lawman. What a joke. The hatred in the man's eyes earlier today had oddly left Cord unaffected. But it was his concern for Maggie being vulnerable to the man's…

Christ. Adrenaline surged through him.

No, Lester wouldn't attack a defenseless woman. And surely the other men weren't interested in her either. Wait. It was the gold that was their target, and Maggie was going to get caught in the cross fire.

Cord grabbed the reins. Red whinnied and stomped angrily at the abrupt interruption. Ignoring the horse's protest, Cord swung into the saddle, checked the rising moon and raced back to Maggie.

SHE STOOD ON THE PORCH, staring out at the gathering darkness, the heaviness in her heart nothing she'd ever known. Not even when her sisters had left, or Pa had passed. Maggie had felt devastatingly sad then, but this cold emptiness was different. Almost as if she were too numb to feel anything more. Maybe because he hadn't bothered to say goodbye.

Her shawl was too light for the bite in the air but she didn't seem to have the energy to go back inside. There wasn't anything in the cabin for her anyway. Not even warmth. Yes, the fire was still going, that's why she knew Cord hadn't been gone long. Foolishly, when she'd first awoken, she'd hoped he'd only made a trip to the barn or the necessary, or had gone outside to bring in more wood.

Her gaze went to the empty corral. Red was gone. So was Cord. She didn't care about Pa's horse. They'd agreed that Cord would take him, but why hadn't he said goodbye? Did he think disappearing would make things easier for her? Tears of anger and frustration burned behind her eyes. She wouldn't be fool enough to actually cry. She'd known all along he'd leave.

She sniffed and used the pole for balance as she slid down to the plank floor. In her haste to dress, she'd foregone her petticoats and could feel the rough unfinished wood poking through her dress and thin drawers. The discomfort was almost welcome. At least she felt something.

Leaning her head back against the pole, she blinked, mildly surprised no tears had fallen. She blinked again, when it appeared that the hazy twilight was playing tricks on her. In the distance, she thought she saw a rider. But it was no trick, she quickly realized. Someone was headed her way.

She struggled to her feet. The rifle sat just inside the door where Cord had left it loaded for her. As she backed toward the door, she squinted at the approaching rider, alarmed at the speed in which he galloped. She prayed it wasn't Lester. Not now. Especially not now.

Could it be Cord?

At the door she hesitated, hope lodged like a nugget in her throat. As the rider got closer, her heart threatened to burst through her chest.

Cord.

He'd come back.

She stepped onto the porch, clutching her shawl so tightly her hands started to cramp. Something was wrong. She felt it deep in her belly even before Cord abruptly reigned in Red and jumped down from the saddle.

"The rifle, Maggie. You need to get it now."

"What's wrong?"

"It's Lester and two other men." He hastily tethered Red. "They're on their way."

"But—" She stopped short when she heard the approach of pounding hooves.

"Maggie, they have torches." He stopped briefly to check his gun. "The rifle. Now."

Torches? Had Lester gone totally mad? She hurried through the door, grabbed the Spencer and joined Cord on the porch.

"Go back inside." He reached for the rifle. "Find the shotgun, even if it's not loaded, but stay inside."

She shook her head. "I know how to use this," she said, bringing the Spencer up to her shoulder to steady her aim.

"Maggie, please."

"No, I won't be bullied any longer. Especially not by the likes of Lester." Her hands were remarkably steady as she watched the three riders stop just beyond the outhouse to light their torches.

Cord moved to stand at her side, though slightly in front of her. "I wish you'd let me handle this," he said. "If anything happened to you—" His voice broke.

She smiled weakly. "You're here. That's enough."

Lester and his men had apparently spotted them. It didn't

seem to matter. The trio continued toward the cabin, the threatening orange glow of their torches held high, though their pace had slowed.

"Stop right there," Maggie called when they got close enough she could see their eyes above the bandanas that hid the rest of their faces. "If you don't think I know who you are, Lester," she said, scornfully emphasizing his name, "then you're even stupider than most people around here seem to think."

"You little bitch—" He lunged forward, but a heavyset man next to him grabbed his shirt, stopping him.

Cord raised his gun.

"Mr. Colbert?" Maggie blinked at the other man she recognized by the missing finger on his left hand. Stunned, she nearly lowered the rifle. "I don't believe it. I used to school your daughter."

He stared down at the ground. "Times have been tough lately. Just give us the gold, Maggie. That's all we want. We're not gonna harm you."

"Unless you make us." Lester waved his torch menacingly.

"I'd sooner blow a hole clean through you than give you one speck of gold dust," she said at the same time Cord cocked his gun.

All three men backed up, and then Lester pulled down his bandana and ground out, "It ain't like I haven't offered to buy the place."

Maggie snorted. "Why is that? What do you think is so valuable about this cabin?" She glanced at the other two men. "Has he told you why he's so interested in driving me away?"

Both men turned to look at the deputy.

"You listen to me, Lester, and you listen good. Pa is dead. This cabin, the gold, the claim, it's all mine now. And even if I were inclined to sell, you'd be the last person in the territory to whom I'd give the opportunity. I'd give it away first.

Now, get off my property before I change my mind about blowing you all the way to California."

A long tense silence lapsed, giving Maggie time to experience a frisson of fear at her boldness. She understood that having Cord by her side had fortified her. But what if he left again? Would she find this kind of courage?

"You ain't seen the last of me, Maggie Dawson," Lester said finally, starting to whirl his horse around. "I reckon the sheriff will be mighty curious about what happened to your pa."

"I have a thing or two to say to the sheriff myself," she responded, keeping the rifle aimed. And right then she knew. She was a different woman than the one who'd run from her own shadow a week ago. She almost smiled.

Lester leaned over and spit in the dirt, and then used the back of his sleeve to wipe his mouth before riding off to join the other two who'd gotten a head start.

Her hands slightly shaky, Maggie lowered the Spencer. It suddenly felt like a hundred pounds.

Cord cupped a warm palm over her shoulder. "You were really something, Maggie Dawson."

"I was," she said, turning to give him a warm smile. "Wasn't I?"

He smiled back. "What am I going to do with you?"

"Take me to Hay Camp."

A FEW MINUTES before sunrise they rode into Hay Camp. The street was deserted but lanterns flickered in shop windows and rowdy noise from a saloon pierced the sleepy morning air. Though she had never complained once, Cord knew Maggie was exhausted by the way she slumped against him, her arms slack around his waist. After stopping halfway to rest, they'd ridden hard trying to beat the snow that seemed to lurk in the dark threatening clouds bearing down on them from the north.

He spotted a hotel on the left, thought briefly about dropping Maggie off there before looking for Reese Winslow, but reconsidered. He doubted Maggie would stand for it. Besides, selfishly, he wanted her with him, whether he found the sister or not.

Nearby someone was brewing coffee. Trying not to disturb Maggie, he shifted in the saddle in an attempt to figure out where the enticing smell was coming from. That's when he saw the doctor's shingle, hanging outside of a small clapboard building next to the boardinghouse.

Cord dug in his heels and urged Red closer, though the windows were dark and he was struck by his foolishness thinking he could ride into town and expect…what…a welcoming committee? Hell, he didn't know what he'd expected, he was dead tired, too. Not that his dream mattered anymore, assuming it had been a message from Masi.

In front of the doctor's office, he reined in the chestnut, and stared up at the cloudy sky. The moon had faded about an hour ago, and along with it, the potential opportunity to return to the future. He didn't care about himself. He'd made his decision the moment he realized Lester was coming after Maggie. But Cord had wanted to find the Winslow women and pass on what he knew.

Which was what exactly? He'd had a dream, that's all. The full moon may have had nothing to do with him returning home. Until last night he'd started to believe that the camera was the key. Not that he had the faintest idea where it was. He was pretty sure it hadn't traveled with him.

He stretched his neck to the side as if the motion would clear the confusion swimming in his head. The dream had to have meant something or Masi wouldn't have appeared, she wouldn't have been so adamant that he get moving last night.

Behind him, Maggie stirred, and though certain she was still asleep, he reassuringly touched her hand tucked between his belly and his arm. In that instant, an astounding thought struck him. Masi's message hadn't been about returning to L.A., it was about Maggie. He understood now. Last night he'd been forced to choose between his old life, and staying with her.

When it had mattered, he'd been forced to admit to himself that he loved Maggie. That he couldn't imagine living without her.

The idea shook him to the core. Was this really love he felt? This unfamiliar feeling that had been simmering inside him for the past two days? It had to be, but how did she feel about him? He knew she was grateful, and that losing her virginity to him was bound to rouse an intimate bond. But did she love him? Was he good enough?

More than anything right now he needed privacy, time to talk to Maggie, to stare into her eyes and learn some truths. He flicked the reins, about to circle back to the hotel, when he thought he saw movement near the office door. Murky light from the overcast sky and a struggling sun still too low to be of much use tricked his vision, but he was pretty sure he saw the silhouette of a woman.

She hesitated, and then stepped out of the shadows, her long pale blond hair a shimmering gold beacon. She wore white nightclothes beneath a wrap similar to Maggie's, and black high-top shoes.

"Reese Winslow?" he asked.

She sighed, sounding weary, surprisingly reluctant. "I was expecting you. It's Reese Keegan now."

"You were *expecting* me?"

Behind him, Maggie stirred against his back. "Cord?" she murmured around a yawn. "Are we there yet?"

He squeezed her hand. "We're here."

"Bet you could use some coffee. Why don't you come in?"

At the sound of Reese's voice, Maggie poked her head around Cord's shoulder. "Hello," she said, clearly startled.

Cord introduced both him and Maggie, and then they followed Reese inside in silence. Reese had said she'd been expecting him. He couldn't wait to hear about that.

Reese lit a couple of lanterns. The room was small and sparse, functional as a waiting room but that was about it. She gestured to a pair of plain oak chairs, started a kettle of coffee and then joined them. "Coffee should be done in a couple of days," she said, smiling ruefully. "There are some things I still really miss."

She and Cord both laughed. Maggie just stared wide-eyed.

"You said you were expecting me," Cord prompted, unable to suppress his curiosity.

Reese nodded slowly. "Two years ago, even with a gun to my head I wouldn't have admitted this, but last night I had a dream about you and I knew you were coming."

Cord straightened. "Was there an older Indian woman in your dream?"

Reese's eyebrows lifted. "Yes."

"And something about the moon being full?"

"I don't think so." Reese frowned. "At least I don't remember. The only thing that seemed significant was that you were from L.A. and were coming to find Ellie and me."

Cord smiled. So he'd been right about his grandmother's message. He could almost feel Masi in the room with them, grinning at him, no doubt pleased with her matchmaking. God, he missed her. "The dream gave me the feeling that last night's full moon was the key to returning home. I figured you had the other piece of the puzzle."

Maggie sat silently, her features tight. They'd traveled fast with scarcely any conversation, and Cord hadn't told her about his dream, or the significance of the full moon. Maybe he should have, but it hadn't seemed important at the time.

"It was the camera that brought Ellie and I here. We know that for sure." Reese studied him. "What about you?"

"It was the camera," he muttered half to himself, thinking back to the fateful moment. "In the old chest in the attic."

"That's right, but I don't understand—" Reese shook her head, clearly bewildered. "The camera was destroyed months ago. Ellie and I both saw it happen."

Cord slumped in the chair. He shouldn't be surprised that the situation kept getting crazier. "Maybe it was a different camera," he said quietly, somehow knowing that wasn't the case.

Reese steadily met his eyes. "The existence of another camera changes nothing for Ellie and me. We're not going back."

He nodded his understanding, and then for the next half hour they somberly compared notes regarding the events that brought them to Deadwood. Cord learned that Ellie Winslow had also married and lived five doors down, and then filled Reese in on news from L.A. She was relieved to discover that her parents were both doing well, and had in fact reconciled and planned to remarry after being divorced for five years. Neither Cord nor Reese mentioned the camera again.

Maggie said nothing. Not while they were at Reese's, nor on the short ride to the hotel. But a thousand questions hung in the air between them, and Cord felt the tension weighing so heavily that he was beginning to sweat. Since he'd first met her, she'd worn her heart on her sleeve, but right now, he had no idea what was going on in her head.

THEY CHECKED INTO the hotel, for propriety's sake, Cord signing them in as husband and wife. A day ago Maggie would've thrilled at simply seeing their names on paper that way, but not now. He looked grim, and she was horribly afraid she wasn't going to like what he had to say.

She'd listened well while Cord and the woman had talked.

Much of what they discussed made no sense to her, but that didn't matter. Only two things stuck out in her mind. The wistful look in Cord's eyes when he'd spoken of the place called L.A., and the hopeful expression on his face when he'd learned that the moon might not be his only way home.

He opened the door to the room and stepped aside to let her go first. "I hope you don't mind that I took only one room, funds being limited and all," he said once he'd closed the door behind them.

That he had to explain the intimacy made her all the more sad. "It's fine." She forced a smile, her gaze straying from the small corner dresser to the double bed. It looked comfortable, unlike the narrow cot in her room. They'd both fit nicely on this bed. The thought brought a lump to her throat.

Hesitantly he took her hand and pressed it between his two warm palms. "We need to talk."

No amount of dread could delay the inevitable, and she gave a jerky nod. She had to be brave, now more than ever. She could never blame him for not wanting to stay, and she couldn't allow him to see the pain his leaving would cause.

"This camera you spoke of," she said calmly. "It has to exist, right? It brought you here. I know Reese said it was destroyed but we can find it. I'll help you. We can use Pa's gold…offer a reward—"

The stark look that settled on his face stopped her cold.

"I don't want your gold, Maggie," he said, tightening his grip on her hand. "I want you."

Her whole body went numb. "You're saying you'll take me with you?" she said slowly.

His brows drew together, and for the first time since she'd met him, she saw fear in his eyes. "I want to stay. Here. With you."

"I don't understand. You rushed to get here while the moon

was full. Then when you learned of the camera you were excited. I saw it in your expression."

He took both her hands and pulled her toward him. "Ah, Maggie. It was relief, not excitement. I thought I had failed Reese and Ellie by not getting here in time. I wanted to give them the opportunity to go home if that's what they wanted." He let go of one hand and brushed the backs of his fingers down her cheek. "I don't care about the gold, the camera or about returning to the future."

Her heartbeat quickened at his tender look.

"I only care about you," he said, and lowered his head to press a soft kiss to her lips. "Only you."

She closed her eyes, praying the moment would never end, and thanking God for sending this man into her life. Never had she felt so safe and warm, and as loath as she was to break the magical spell, one thing still troubled her. She looked up at him. "I'm worried about why Mary never responded."

"I was thinking about that myself. I doubt Lester intercepted your letters because he would've known about your father. How reliable is mail delivery?"

"I'm not sure. Although I have received late posts from both her and Clara before."

"Don't worry. We'll find her." He ran a soothing hand down her back and kissed the top of her head. "Today we'll get some sleep. Tomorrow we'll return home to pack a few things."

"Home?" Coming from him, the single word filled her with indescribable joy.

"For now," he told her, his mouth curving in a bone-melting smile. "I can't wait to show you the ocean, Maggie."

"Oh, yes, I want very much to see it. Maybe we could even stay in San Francisco for a while?"

"Any place you want, we'll call home."

Maggie's breath caught, and she uttered the words she had never said to another living soul. "I love you."

Cord tightened his hold. "I love you, Maggie Dawson, and I promise to spend every day trying to make you the happiest woman on earth."

* * * * *

In honor of our 60th anniversary, Harlequin® American Romance® is celebrating by featuring an all-American male each month, all year long with
MEN MADE IN AMERICA!
This June, we'll be featuring American men living in the West.

Here's a sneak preview of
THE CHIEF RANGER by Rebecca Winters.

Chief Ranger Vance Rossiter has to confront the sister of a man who died while under Vance's watch...and also confront his attraction to her.

"Chief Ranger Rossiter?" The sight of the woman who'd stepped inside Vance's office brought him to his feet. "I'm Rachel Darrow. Your secretary said I should come right in."

"Please," he said, walking around his desk to shake her hand. At a glance he estimated she was in her midtwenties. Her feminine curves did wonders for the pale blue T-shirt and jeans she was wearing. "Ranger Jarvis informed me there's a young boy with you."

The unfriendly expression in her beautiful green eyes caught him off guard. "Yes," was her clipped reply. "When we arrived in Yosemite the ranger told me I couldn't go anywhere in the park until I talked to you first."

"That's right."

"Knowing you wanted this meeting to be private, he offered to show my nephew around Headquarters."

So this woman was the victim's sister…. "What's his name?"

"Nicky."

The boy who haunted Vance's dreams now had a name. "How old is he?"

"He turned six three weeks ago. Were you the man in charge when my brother and sister-in-law were killed?"

"Yes. To tell you I'm sorry for what happened couldn't begin to convey my feelings."

The woman's gaze didn't flicker. "I won't even try to describe mine. Just tell me one thing. Was their accident preventable?"

"Yes," he answered without hesitation.

"In other words, the people working under you fell asleep on your watch and two lives were snuffed out as a result."

Hearing it put like that, he had to set the record straight. "My staff had nothing to do with it. I, myself, could have prevented the loss of life."

Ms. Darrow's expression hardened. "So you admit culpability."

"Yes. I take full blame."

A look of pain crossed over her features. "You can just stand there and admit it?" Her cry echoed that of his own tortured soul.

"Yes." He sucked in his breath.

"I work for a cruise line. Aboard ship, it's the captain's responsibility to maintain rigid safety regulations. If a disaster like that had happened while he was in charge he would have been relieved of his command and never given another ship again."

Rachel Darrow couldn't know she was preaching to the converted. "If you've come to the park with the intention of bringing a lawsuit against me for negligence, maybe you should." It would only be what he deserved.

"Maybe I will."

In the next instant, she wheeled around and hurried out of his office. Vance could have gone after her, but it would cause a scene, something he was loath to do for a variety of reasons.

In the first place, he needed to cool down before he approached her again.

The discovery of the Darrows' frozen bodies had affected every ranger in the park. A little boy had been orphaned—a boy whose aunt was all he had left.

* * * * *

Will Rachel allow Vance to explain—and will she
let him into her heart?
Find out in
THE CHIEF RANGER
Available June 2009 from Harlequin®
American Romance®.

We'll be spotlighting a different series every month
throughout 2009 to celebrate our 60th anniversary.

Look for Harlequin®
American Romance® in June!

Join us for a year-long celebration of the rugged
American male! From cops to cowboys—
Men Made in America has the hero
you've been dreaming about!

Look for

The Chief Ranger

by Rebecca Winters, on sale in June!

www.eHarlequin.com

HARBPA09

nocturne™

New York Times Bestselling Author

REBECCA BRANDEWYNE

FROM THE MISTS OF WOLF CREEK

Hallie Muldoon suspects that her grandmother
has special abilities, but her sudden death
forces Hallie to return to Wolf Creek, where
details emerge of a spell cast. Local farmer
Trace Coltrane and the wolf that prowls around
the farmhouse both appear out of nowhere, and
a killer has Hallie in his sights. With no other
choice, Hallie relies on Trace for help,
not knowing if the mysterious Trace is a
mesmerizing friend or a deadly foe....

Available June wherever books are sold.

REQUEST YOUR FREE BOOKS!

2 FREE NOVELS
PLUS 2
FREE GIFTS!

HARLEQUIN®

Blaze

Red-hot reads!

YES! Please send me 2 FREE Harlequin® Blaze™ novels and my 2 FREE gifts (gifts are worth about $10). After receiving them, if I don't wish to receive any more books, I can return the shipping statement marked "cancel". If I don't cancel, I will receive 6 brand-new novels every month and be billed just $4.24 per book in the U.S. or $4.71 per book in Canada. Shipping and handling is just 25¢ per book. That's a savings of 15% or more off the cover price! I understand that accepting the 2 free books and gifts places me under no obligation to buy anything. I can always return a shipment and cancel at any time. Even if I never buy another book, the two free books and gifts are mine to keep forever.

151 HDN ERVA 351 HDN ERUX

Name	(PLEASE PRINT)	
Address		Apt. #
City	State/Prov.	Zip/Postal Code

Signature (if under 18, a parent or guardian must sign)

Mail to the **Harlequin Reader Service:**
IN U.S.A.: P.O. Box 1867, Buffalo, NY 14240-1867
IN CANADA: P.O. Box 609, Fort Erie, Ontario L2A 5X3

Not valid to current subscribers of Harlequin Blaze books.

Want to try two free books from another line?
Call 1-800-873-8635 or visit www.morefreebooks.com.

* Terms and prices subject to change without notice. Prices do not include applicable taxes. N.Y. residents add applicable sales tax. Canadian residents will be charged applicable provincial taxes and GST. Offer not valid in Quebec. This offer is limited to one order per household. All orders subject to approval. Credit or debit balances in a customer's account(s) may be offset by any other outstanding balance owed by or to the customer. Please allow 4 to 6 weeks for delivery. Offer available while quantities last.

Your Privacy: Harlequin Books is committed to protecting your privacy. Our Privacy Policy is available online at www.eHarlequin.com or upon request from the Reader Service. From time to time we make our lists of customers available to reputable third parties who may have a product or service of interest to you. If you would prefer we not share your name and address, please check here. ☐

HB09R

Silhouette *Desire*

MAN of the MONTH

USA TODAY bestselling author

ANN MAJOR

THE BRIDE HUNTER

Former marine turned P.I. Connor Storm
is hired to find the long-lost Golden Spurs
heiress, Rebecca Collins, aka Anna Barton.
Once Connor finds her, desire takes over and
he marries her within two weeks! On their
wedding night he reveals he knows her true
identity and she flees. When he finds her
again, can he convince her that the love they
share is worth fighting for?

**Available June
wherever books are sold.**

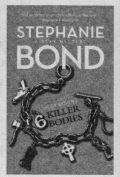

You're invited to join our Tell Harlequin Reader Panel!

By joining our new reader panel you will:

- Receive Harlequin® books—they are FREE and yours to keep with no obligation to purchase anything!
- Participate in fun online surveys
- Exchange opinions and ideas with women just like you
- Have a say in our new book ideas and help us publish the best in women's fiction

In addition, you will have a chance to win great prizes and receive special gifts! See Web site for details. Some conditions apply. Space is limited.

To join, visit us at
www.TellHarlequin.com.

HARLEQUIN *Blaze*

COMING NEXT MONTH

Available May 26, 2009

#471 BRANDED Tori Carrington
Jo Atchison isn't your average cowgirl. She's rough, she's tough and she's sexy as hell. And regardless of the rules, she wants rancher Trace Armstrong. Luckily, Trace wants Jo, too. The only one not happy about it is Jo's volatile boyfriend....

#472 WHEN THE SUN GOES DOWN... Crystal Green
A trip to Japan on family business is just the chance Juliana Thompsen and Tristan Cole have been waiting for. They've been hopelessly in love with each other for years, but a family feud made a relationship impossible. Now they're alone, and they're going to experience *everything* they've missed. But will it be enough to last them a lifetime?

#473 UNDRESSED Heather MacAllister
Encounters
Take some naughty talk, add one *very* thin wall between the last dressing room in a bridal shop and a tuxedo boutique, and what do you have? The recipe for a happy marriage...and four very satisfied—and enlightened—couples. When you get this kind of tailoring, who needs a honeymoon?

#474 TWIN TEMPTATION Cara Summers
The Wrong Bed: Again and Again
Maddie Farrell has just learned she has a twin sister. And she's an heiress. *And* she's just had sex with the hot stranger in her bed! It must be a mistake. Right? Hmm—she might have to have more sex just to make sure....

#475 LETTERS FROM HOME Rhonda Nelson
Uniformly Hot!
Ranger Levi McPherson is getting some anonymous, red-hot love letters during his tour of duty! When he comes home on leave, he's determined to track down the mysterious author...and show her that actions speak louder than words.

#476 THE MIGHTY QUINNS: BRODY Kate Hoffmann
Quinns Down Under
Runaway bride Payton Harwell thinks she's hit rock bottom when she ends up in jail—in Australia! But then sexy rebel Brody Quinn bails her out and lets her into his home, his bed, his life. Only, Payton's past isn't as far away as she thinks it is....

www.eHarlequin.com

HBCNMBPA0509